TAUL LAUME

THE LONE RANGER
and the Mystery Ranch

The Lone Ranger Stories

Written by

FRAN STRIKER

and based on the famous
Lone Ranger adventures
created by

GEO. W. TRENDLE

THE LONE RANGER

THE LONE RANGER AND THE MYSTERY RANCH

THE LONE RANGER AND THE GOLD ROBBERY

THE LONE RANGER AND THE OUTLAW STRONG-
HOLD

THE LONE RANGER AND TONTO

THE LONE RANGER AT THE HAUNTED GULCH

THE LONE RANGER TRAPS THE SMUGGLERS

THE LONE RANGER RIDES AGAIN

THE LONE RANGER RIDES NORTH

THE LONE RANGER AND THE SILVER BULLET

THE LONE RANGER ON POWDERHORN TRAIL

THE LONE RANGER IN WILD HORSE CANYON

The Lone Ranger
and the Mystery Ranch

Written by FRAN STRIKER

and based on the famous *Lone Ranger* adventures

created by GEO. W. TRENDLE

GROSSET & DUNLAP *Publishers*

NEW YORK

CONTENTS

THE LONE RANGER
and the Mystery Ranch

CHAPTER I

DEAD MAN'S VALLEY

Silence, intense and oppressive, gripped the moonlit expanse of plain. No living thing stirred, and there were no trees whose foliage might rustle. It was as if the hand of Death had reached out to touch all that was capable of sound or motion. Clouds hung low, blocking out all light from moon and stars. Absorbed heat, given off by the far reaches of level land, made a depressing atmosphere.

Then through the night, two men moved at a slow gait. Their horses were two silvery-white blobs without definite outline at ten yards distant. The men sat their horses with an easy grace, but with the constant vigilance of those whose life might be forfeit for a moment's relaxation.

The smaller of the men had the bronzed, high-cheekboned face of an Indian. His long, black hair was parted in the center of his head and drawn back tightly to be fashioned in a war-knot at the back of his neck. The Indian's name was Tonto, and he was the faithful friend and ally of the most mysterious figure ever to ride the plains and prairies, or roam the woods and mountains of the west. He was known as "The Lone Ranger."

"Maybe we find-um place for camp soon," he said.

His companion did not answer at once. His very silence seemed a part of his grim strength, dominating personality and strong character. His was the lithe grace of a panther. Broad of shoulder, lean of hip, his six-feet-two of height was topped by a broad-brimmed Stetson.

The upper part of his clean-shaven face was masked. A fine, firm chin and well-formed mouth added to the impression that here was a man of sterling courage and untold power. The ivory handles of a brace of 45's protruded from holsters strapped low on either side.

"We'll push on a little longer, Tonto," he said at last.

The Indian looked at him across the few feet of space that separated the horses. There seemed no reason for continuing further. Both white stallions were worn from the hard trail of the past sixteen hours.

"There are trees ahead, where we can make a better camp," the masked man finished.

Necessity and constant vigilance made it a habit of the Lone Ranger to keep himself informed about the terrain. He never missed an opportunity to add to his fund of knowledge. When he once passed over a certain stretch of country, he would never forget its hills and valleys, woods and water, arroyos and rock formations. Many times in the past, his safety had depended upon this uncanny knowledge. He might at any moment be in desperate need of a place of concealment.

His daring acts of courage in the name of Justice made him known throughout the West. To many of the pioneers he existed as an almost legendary character. Only a small portion of those who knew of him had seen him, and none of these had ever seen his face unmasked.

Many times, his safety had depended upon his knowledge of a cave or other place of hiding. Many outlaws had sworn to kill the masked rider for his work in bringing countless desperadoes to justice and breaking up untold rustling gangs and outlaw bands.

Even lawmen wanted the Lone Ranger. Only a few had been convinced that this strange figure was not an outlaw, and those few thanked God for the man who had no thought of personal glory or reward ... for the man whose only purpose in life seemed to be to help the deserving and punish the lawless in a region where laws were few and those few, seldom enforced.

Tonto peered ahead into the gloom. Only the soft clump of the horses' hoofs broke the absolute stillness of the night. Trees ahead, but how far?

There were no stars visible to aid in charting a course across the unbroken plain, but the Lone Ranger seemed instinctively to head in the right direction. "There is a little valley, somewhere ahead of us," he told his friend, "and if we don't find water in the valley, there are trees beyond. We can camp there." He didn't suspect the dread thing he'd find in the valley, and he didn't know that at that very moment, hooded men broke through the trees he mentioned, carrying death and destruction where they went.

It was half an hour before they reached the slight depression of the valley. The stillness here was even more marked than on the open plain. There were a few trees whose cool leaves at times brushed the bodies of the masked man and the Indian, but no breath of air stirred the leaves, to make the slightest rustle. The valley seemed an eerie place, with only the soft clump of hoofs to break the deathlike stillness.

A queer sensation crept down the Lone Ranger's spine. He felt a foreboding of evil, an unexplainable sense of a Presence in the valley. Something seemed to be there with them! Yet there was no sound. The horses too felt something unusual. Though no command was given, either by voice or rein, they slowed their pace until they barely moved ahead.

A shaft of light struck down as the moon broke through the clouds for a moment. The Lone Ranger, jerked quickly on the reins, to bring Silver to a willing halt. The pale light reflected from the face of a man directly ahead and slightly above the Lone Ranger.

It was a distorted face, with wide-staring eyes, and open mouth. The head was twisted to one side and sweat had streaked the dirt to make it a grim and awful object.

The man was dead!

A rope dropping from the branch above his head was formed into a tight noose about his swollen throat. His feet dangled free and clear.

Quickly urging his horse a couple paces forward, the Lone Ranger circled the lifeless body with one arm, while Tonto slashed through the rope with a knife. Then the Indian dismounted and helped lower the rigid form to the ground. The moon was gone again. Darkness shrouded the valley.

While the masked man brought a candle from his saddle bag and stuck it in the ground beside the corpse, Tonto struck a match and lit it. By the poor illumination, they examined the pitiful victim of some cruel hangman.

The figure on the ground was that of a young man. He couldn't have been more than twenty-five years old. Alive, his face might have been considered good-looking, in a homespun sort of way. His features were well shaped, and the red hair and freckles made the Lone Ranger think of several good-natured, easy-going fellows of similar appearance. But now his face was transformed by the torture he must have suffered before death came.

While the Lone Ranger searched the dead man's pockets for some identifying mark, Tonto lighted a second candle and by its light, examined the ground on his hands and knees. He saw that horsemen had been here, quite a few of them, to judge by the way the grass was beaten down. The Indian was sure they must be outlaws, because a legal execution would not have been performed in this place so far from any town or village. Then his hand brushed something on the ground. He examined it more closely and found that it was a black, cloth hood, shaped to cover a man's head, with two holes cut out where the eyes would be. This hood was not an unfamiliar article to Tonto. In fact, it was altogether *too* familiar. It represented "The Night Legion."

The Lone Ranger nodded when he saw the hood. He, too, knew of the Night Legion. Holding out a bit of paper for his Indian friend to see, he said, "This was fastened to the dead man's shirt." He held it closer to the light, while Tonto studied it.

"What note say?"

"A man who sees the face of one of the Night Legion, dies!"

Tonto nodded grimly.

"That hood explains it. This fellow met the Night Legion here, and there was a struggle. He managed to tear the hood off one of them, and because of it was killed."

"Ugh," agreed the Indian. Then he dropped suddenly beside the still form on the ground. The right hand of the dead man was clenched about something that had so far escaped notice. Prying apart the rigid fingers, Tonto found a stub of pencil and another scrap of paper. It was the torn, stiff back of what had once been a small notebook. Holding it close to the candlelight, the Indian and masked man saw the hurriedly scribbled words.

"Good Lord," breathed the Lone Ranger, "that fellow had sterling courage. While he strangled, waiting for that rope to choke his life away, he managed to write this in the hope someone would find it."

"What say?"

"Joe," said the Lone Ranger, studying the ragged letters, "Joe Frisby shack . . . in woods . . . two miles west."

CHAPTER II

THE NIGHT LEGION

Digging, with the few tools the Lone Ranger and Tonto carried with them, was arduous toil, but the poor lad, whose bruised and battered body still lay on the soft grass, could not be left exposed to the ravages of wolves and buzzards. For a time, the Lone Ranger thought of carrying the dead man with him to the nearest town, in the hope of finding relatives or friends, but the nearest town was many miles away, and just ahead, according to the dead man's message, there was a man named Joe Frisby, and a warning of danger.

The Night Legion was near by, and sooner or later the Lone Ranger knew he'd meet these fiends. He'd planned it, in fact, he'd dedicated his life to that meeting that was sure to come. It might be tonight, tomorrow, or it might be many months, but when he *did* meet them, he'd need all the strength of his horse, unhampered by a second man in the saddle.

The shallow grave was finally prepared, and the body, wrapped in one of the Lone Ranger's blankets, was gently lowered to its final resting place. Then, hat in hand, the Lone Ranger did a rare thing. In the darkness, he removed his mask. For an instant, while his clean-cut face was lifted toward the sky in silent

8

prayer for the departed soul, and while Tonto's head was bowed, the moon again broke through the clouds. Tonto echoed the white man's "Amen."

The two filled in the grave and packed the dirt down. They marked the place with a crude cross made of greenwood lashed together. Wood from the same tree that had served so grim a purpose a short while before.

When they finished, the Lone Ranger said, "One more added to the many marks against the Night Legion."

Tonto nodded silent agreement. The horses were repacked, tools stowed in place, and candles returned to the saddle bags. Then the two men swung to their saddles.

Soon the valley was behind them, and the horses slowed down as the Lone Ranger and Tonto entered a small woods. "We've covered about two miles," the masked man said. "I wonder just what was meant by the name Joe Frisby?"

There was no need for reply from Tonto. No time for one, in fact. At that moment, the Lone Ranger brought Silver to a halt. "Look through the trees."

A dim, red glow, barely visible ahead, resolved itself into the embers of a fire. Approaching closer, the Lone Ranger saw a fireplace, through the open door of what proved to be a small, one-room cabin.

"You," said the masked man to his friend, "stay here with the horses. I'm going ahead on foot."

Tonto started to object. When there was danger,

he wanted to be at his tall, masked friend's side. "It's best," went on the Lone Ranger, "for you to keep back. In case someone gets the drop on me, you can come from behind and cover them. If we're there together, we'd have no chance."

Tonto saw the good sense in the plan. "You call," he said, speaking in a voice hardly above a whisper, "Me come."

The Lone Ranger went ahead. His movement was as silent as that of a mountain lion. No twigs snapped beneath his feet. He carefully tested each step, shifting his weight from one foot to the other slowly. "The Night Legion," he thought. They were near here. Was Joe Frisby one of them, or was Joe Frisby in danger at their hands? Was it a genuine note in the dead man's hand, or was it merely part of a carefully laid trap to bring the Lone Ranger into the hands of the Night Legion?

Countless thoughts raced through his active mind as he drew closer to the shack. The door was open wide, and there seemed to be no movement inside.

The evidence of sheer brutality, ruthless destruction and a cold-blooded attempt at murder, earmarked another outrage of the Night Legion.

The only thing left undisturbed in the small cabin was the remnant of a fire. Embers still glowed in the fireplace to cast a dim, uncertain light about the room itself. Hands held less than a scant inch from the ivory butts of his six guns, the Lone Ranger stepped into the room. A quick glance showed no one crouch-

ing behind the door, or tensed in a dim corner, ready
to leap upon him. Near the crude bunk against the
wall on the masked man's right, a white-haired old
man sprawled in a lifeless, unnatural position on the
floor.

Keeping one hand near a gun, the masked man
lighted a stub of candle which was on the floor beside
the upset table, and held it high to survey the scene in
more detail. There was even more destruction than his
first quick glance disclosed. Furniture, crude though
it was, had been torn apart in wanton destruction.
Several boards were ripped from the floor to disclose
the hard-packed dirt beneath. An old trunk, standing in one corner, had its lid smashed open, and the
contents, consisting of an assorted batch of clothing,
old letters, papers, some mining certificates, and other
miscellaneous odds and ends, were strewn about the
place.

It seemed as though nothing in the one-room shack
had gone untouched. Even the fireplace stones had
been attacked by the old running iron that apparently
served as a poker. Several of the stones lay on the floor
where they'd fallen after being dug from place.

The quick eye and keen mind of the Lone Ranger
observed all these things in the half minute he stood in
the center of the room with the candle held high. Then
he moved quickly to the sprawling figure on the floor
beside the bed. Placing his light beside the old man's
snow-white head, the Lone Ranger's strong, yet gentle
hands explored the unconscious man.

By all the laws of nature, Joe Frisby should have been already stiffening in death. The knife thrust in his back was in a bad place. Dark moisture still seeped from the wound to spread out on the floor. And yet, Joe Frisby breathed. His breathing came in labored gasps, but his weak heartbeat seemed regular.

"If Tonto were only here," he thought, "he could do more for this man than I." Tonto's skill in treating knife and pistol wounds was nothing short of miraculous. He seemed to combine the white man's surgery with the ancient lore of his own people, and many a man lived in the West, only because it was Tonto who had cared for him when he came out on the losing end of a gun fight.

The Lone Ranger, himself, was one of these. While he cut away the man's shirt, built up the fire, and put water over it to heat, he recalled the vivid impressions of his first meeting with the Indian. "The Night Legion" he muttered, in thinking of that time, long months ago. He breathed the words as if they were a curse. Indeed, the Night Legion had been for some time a curse to the law-abiding settlers in the cattle country.

It was to wipe out the dreaded, hooded riders who were banded together in outlawry of every sort, that a small band of Texas Rangers had ridden into the district. Then, through the betrayal of a man the Rangers had befriended, the Night Legion surrounded them in their camp. Expert killers, sighting their guns from behind protecting rocks, poured a withering fire on the surprised lawmen. The fight was hard, and the Texas Rangers made a game stand, but unprotected as they were, they had no chance for victory against huge odds.

To a man, the Texas Rangers fell, while their horses were led away by gloating, laughing murderers in black hoods. Recollection of that fight brought hard lines to the masked man. He tested the water with his finger, and decided it was warm enough to bathe Joe Frisby's wound. While he withdrew the knife as gently as possible and proceeded to bathe the ugly gash between the narrow shoulders, he wondered if some strange fate hadn't been the cause of his own salvation.

Some Fate that had brought Tonto, the Indian, to the scene of the Texas Ranger Massacre; fate that had left him, of all the Texas Rangers, with a spark of life in his badly shattered body. Tonto had carried him in his brawny arms to a cave, where careful treatment healed the wounds and brought the Ranger back to health. "The only one of the Texas Rangers" he'd thought at the time. "The Lone Ranger."

Then, knowing that the Night Legionnaires would mark him as a Texas Ranger if they saw his face, he masked it. His one mission in life was to avenge the death of all his comrades, and wipe out the cursed menace that seemed to have grown steadily in power since the battle. No one knew him, as he and Tonto searched the country for the key men of the Night Legion. Many a time, in their search, they'd found a chance to aid the cause of justice, and these occasions interrupted their main objective.

No one but Tonto knew his true background, and even Tonto didn't know his name.

Joe Frisby stirred slightly when the Lone Ranger finished tying a bandage in place. The wound seemed to have just missed a fatal spot. There was a lump on Old Joe's head, the result of a blow that might in itself have caused unconsciousness.

"Not as good a job as Tonto would have done," he mused, as he knotted the dressing, "but it will stop the bleeding."

Once more the old man moved slightly.

"Take it easy," the deep voice murmured, "take it easy, Joe, you're going to be all right."

The old man's eyelids fluttered and for a moment he looked wide-eyed at the masked face close to his. "I'm awake," he wheezed, "yuh murderin' sidewinder." Then Joe's eyes closed again. He moaned softly. There was a lot of spunk in him, despite his wounds.

Tucked beneath the mattress on the bunk, the Lone Ranger saw the protruding end of a flask. He took it, unscrewed the cap, and smelled it. "Brandy," he muttered. "It might be the very thing for him right now."

He held Joe Frisby's head up slightly, and poured a little of the strong liquor between the bearded lips. Old Joe gulped as the brandy burned down his throat and took hold. Then he swallowed another draught, coughed slightly, and once more opened his eyes.

CHAPTER III

JOE FRISBY'S STORY

"Whew!" Joe Frisby gasped and coughed with the brandy given him by the Lone Ranger. It seemed to bring him new life, as he tried to sit erect without the support of the masked man's arm behind his head. His eyes were pale and blue, and somewhat dazed for the moment. Then, as he saw more clearly the one who crouched beside him, he squinted slightly, and a light of bitter hatred crossed his face.

"Why'd yuh come back?" he rasped. "Ain't yuh satisfied with what yuh got?" He paused for breath, and his face settled into bitter lines as the extent of his loss struck him. "My money belt an' the map . . . gone!" he muttered. "The map! Blast it all, if I had it back, I'd swap it for a gun with just one ca'tridge in it!"

"To shoot me with?" the masked man queried with a half smile on his lips. He was well pleased at the old fellow's returning vigor, and tolerant of his mistake in thinking the Lone Ranger one of the outlaws who had attacked him. His voice was kind, as he continued, "I'm glad you haven't a gun, because you'd only be sorry for what you did with it."

"Sorry!" Frisby exploded. "What do you mean,

15

sorry? None o' the men in these parts would be sorry
tuh git one o' yuh night-ridin' masked snakes that
don't give decent folk a chunce tuh defend themselves."
He sank back exhausted in the supporting arm of the
masked man, and the silence was unbroken for a
minute save for the painful breathing of the wounded
man. Then his eyes flickered open again, and a gleam
of speculation came into them as he fixed his gaze on
the quiet man beside him.

"Say, now I think of it," he muttered, "why did yuh
try tuh kill me one minute, then bring me around to
life the next? What's the idea?" A wry smile twisted
his face. "Plan tuh take me to the rest o' your gang an'
torture me? That's what you rats usually do!"

"Considering everything, I don't wonder you're
pretty much confused. But take it easy for a couple
more minutes, then we'll be able to talk." It was a
soothing voice the Lone Ranger used. The same voice
he used so often in speaking to Silver.

"The night isn't getting any younger," he continued,
"and there are lots of things to be talked over."

"Who be you, stranger?" the old man wheezed out.
"I can't figure it. You wear a mask an' so do they, an'
yet yuh save my life!" A puzzled frown creased his
forehead.

"A masked man," he repeated. "Accordin' tuh my
notions, a man that wears a mask has somethin' tuh
hide."

"I have nothing to hide," the Lone Ranger replied
calmly. "You'll just have to take me as I am. I'm not

one of the Night Legion." He thought it best to make no mention of the dead man, the man who's warning brought him here. He studied Joe Frisby's face when he mentioned the Night Legion, but the words didn't seem to register. He knew the men who came here had been searching the cabin for something that was hard to find. There were countless things he wanted to ask Joe Frisby, but first, the aged man must be made to trust him. When Frisby pondered the last remarks of the Lone Ranger, there was silence.

Joe half extended his large knuckled hand, then withdrew it. He was considering the stranger with a calculating eye. After all, it was this stranger who had saved his life, why not trust him further? When he spoke it was slowly. "Mister," he said, "I reckon yuh'll do. If yuh c'n overlook a couple things I called yuh a while back, I'd admire tuh shake yer hand. My name's Frisby, Joe Frisby."

He again extended his hand, and this time it met that of the Lone Ranger.

"I'm glad to know you, Joe."

"Well," Joe asked, "What's yore handle? What am I s'posed tuh call yuh? Bein' as yore masked, I don't spose you'll tell me your name?" There was a half-expectant note in his voice.

"Why not call me 'Friend'," the masked man answered simply. "I'll take it as a compliment, and I'll come when I'm called."

"Suits me," Frisby said tersely.

The mystery rider sat on the edge of the low bunk

and leaned forward to rest his elbows on his knees. His voice was sharp and clear as he talked. "Now then, let's find out what we can about the men who called on you. They seem to have done quite a bit of damage."

The old fellow sat up abruptly, rage distorting his face as he looked about him at the disordered room. "The ornery coyotes didn't give me a chance!" he growled. "They busted through the door sudden-like, with their heads covered. I seen right off it was the murderous gang of thieves that's been around these parts lately and has got themselves knowed as the Night Legion."

The Lone Ranger nodded grimly. He knew too much about the desperate, hard-riding, ruthless killers.

"They come through the door," Frisby recollected, "an' two of 'em come fer me while the others went fer everything in the room."

He tried to rise, but a sharp pain in his back brought a grimace to his wrinkled face and he sat back on the floor, bracing his shoulder against the edge of the bunk. "I dunno how they knowed about the map," he went on, after a pause, "but they did, an' they tried tuh make me tell where it was hid."

So it was a map for which the Night Legion searched the place. Joe eyed the half empty flask with a wistful look, and ran his tongue across his thin, colorless lips. He glanced at the Lone Ranger, who gave no sign of taking the unvoiced hint. There were questions the masked man would have asked, but he felt the best way to get the story was in Joe Frisby's own style. The questions could come later.

"While the two batted me around, tryin' tuh make me talk, the others went at things, as you c'n see. They ripped the trunk apart, an' the floor up, an' tried tuh take the fireplace down, suspectin' a hidin' place somewhere behind the stones. Then one of 'em suggested mebbe they was holler legs in the chairs or table, so they ripped them apart. Then they finally slit the mattress of my bunk, an' that's where I'd hid the map." He paused for a long moment, to gain new strength before continuing. "Half a map, is what I should say, because that's all it was."

"Half a map?"

"Yere, that's all!" A puzzled look came into his face. "I dunno how they found out about it. It beats me."

"Who knew about it?"

"Two men in the world. I'm one, t'other was my pardner."

"Was the map of any value?"

Joe Frisby nodded slowly. "That map, the two parts of it put tuhgether, was wuth a heap of money. My pardner had one half an' I had t'other half. It had all the information that was needed, tuh make men rich."

"So they found the half of the map in your mattress," the Lone Ranger primed the old man to get his story continued.

"Yep. Then one of 'em come at me with a knife, an' another fetched me a whack on the head, an that's all I c'n rec'lect."

"The men's heads were covered with black cloth, weren't they?"

Joe Frisby nodded. "I suppose, as long as you know this much, I may's well tell the rest, but all this talk is sort of tirin' to me."

"I understand, Joe, but if you'll let me, I might be able to help you." The Lone Ranger still refrained from telling of the dead man he and Tonto found.

"From what you said, pardner, I reckon maybe you know somethin' o' these critturs that make up the Night Legion."

The masked man's mouth was compressed into a thin line. "The more we learn of them," he stated, "the better the chance to wipe them out."

"Just so. Well, I can't tell no more of them. But how they got to know about that half of a map is a downright deep mystery."

Once more the Lone Ranger asked, "What was the map?"

"Well, after some years of prospectin'," Joe related, "my pard an' me had a streak of uncommon good luck. We stumbled on a vein of gold back in the hills that looked to be as rich as any mine that had been found. The ore was as rich as the famous 'Lost Dutchman' mine was said to be, but it was all hard rock minin' that had to be done an' we couldn't afford tuh work it." The words came in a rush that made him pause to gather strength again. Then he continued.

"We made a map of the place so's we could find it again, then we tore the map in half an' my pardner took half an' I kept half. Sam Whitcomb, that's my pard, was tuh go East with his half tuh git backin'. I come here tuh wait fer him, promisin' to wait till he come back. I ain't said a word o' what we found tuh anyone," he went on painfully, "an' tonight, yuh seen what happened."

Old Joe cleared his throat, and looked longingly at the brandy. He decided at another try. "So much talkin' is sort o' hard after hardly sayin' a word for the three years I bin here," he said longingly.

The masked one, a whimsical smile tugging at the corner of his mouth, passed over the flask without a word. Frisby grasped at it eagerly, and shook it with an apologetic gesture. He placed it to his lips and took a long draught, the Adam's apple in his skinny neck moving up and down, as the brandy burned down his throat.

"It's been a powerful long time since I needed liquor like now, pardner. There's been plenty of times when I've drunk a durn sight more an' needed it a durn sight less."

"Frisby, this gang of men that has been terrorizing the entire region must be wiped out completely. No one knows who the leader is, but he is some man that has an uncanny knack of getting information, just as he got the information about your half of the map. I was hoping to learn more about the Night Legion."

"You?"

"Yes."

"You know about the pole-cats?"

"I know that unless they are wiped out soon, they'll undo all that has been done to conquer and civilize the West." The Lone Ranger's voice was broken slightly with the emotion that shook him when he continued. "The Night Legion represents the worst in everything that's ruthless, cruel, brutal and lawless. There are a hundred murders to be paid for, thousands of stolen dollars to be returned . . ."

"An' my map!" Joe Frisby finished with emphasis.

"Tell me," said the Lone Ranger, leaning forward eagerly, "if you heard the voice of the leader of those men."

"I sure did. I heard it aplenty."

"Would you recognize it if you were to hear it again?"

"I'd recognize that voice in Hades, an' what's more, I'd almost be willin' tuh go there tuh git the skunk that owns it."

Joe Frisby spat on the board floor to punctuate his declaration. The Lone Ranger thought he might find a valuable witness in the old man, when the Night Legion was finally brought to trial.

But at that moment, a black blob appeared outside the window. The now brightly burning fire illumined it, and the two eyes peering from behind the holes in the hood looked almost spectral. Joe, reaching once again for the flask, glanced up, and his hand froze halfway to his lips.

Seeing his expression, the Lone Ranger understood. He leaped from the bunk, to spring quickly to one side. His hands flashed down and up, and three shots blasted the silence. Orange flames lashed through the glass window from each of the Ranger's heavy guns, but he'd fired while in mid-air in his leap, and the black hood against the black of night outside, made an uncertain target.

Of the three shots, but one found its mark. A soft moan from Joe Frisby and he rolled over on the floor, the flask dropping from his lifeless fingers. His hand clawed feebly at his chest, and then flopped limp. Directly over his heart, a red smear moistened his denim shirt. This time, there would be no awakening for the old man.

But the Lone Ranger raced through the door. The Night Legion had struck again, another murder to be paid for!

Running through the trees, the Lone Ranger paid no heed to silence. He heard the fading of a horse's hoofs and his only thought as he raced toward Tonto and the horses, was to get aboard the mighty Silver and pursue the hooded killer.

In a fraction of the time it had taken him to reach the house, he was at the tree to which the horses had been tethered. Then it struck him with the force of a blow. Why hadn't those shots brought Tonto? Silver stood alone. Tonto's horse, and Tonto himself, were gone.

CHAPTER IV

The Outlaw Camp

Uncertainty gripped the Lone Ranger as he stood beside his great white stallion in the almost total darkness. Tonto might be close by, somewhere in the weedy tangle. He might be bound and gagged, he might be badly wounded, he might even be dead. To delay and hunt for Tonto would take many precious minutes, when every second counted. There might yet be time to overtake the hooded murderer of old Joe Frisby. The receding sound of the outlaw's horse still came faintly to the masked man's ear.

If Tonto had *not* been attacked by the outlaws, he would have come on the run at the sound of gunfire in the cabin. Tonto would certainly not have left on his own accord, without leaving some sign or message. "A message," thought the tall man. "I haven't even looked." He quickly felt for the saddle, then slid his hand along the tie strings, and there, he felt a bit of paper. His spirits rose on the instant. The paper wasn't there when he'd left Silver. This had to be a message from Tonto.

He struck a match and, cupping it in one hand, made out the crudely blocked letters. "See trail," he read.

24

He recalled Tonto's animal-like ability to penetrate the darkness when his senses were keyed to a high pitch. "Go hunt men." So Tonto had left of his own accord, to follow a trail through the cottonwoods in the hope of locating the outlaws' camp. The better part of half an hour had been spent with old Joe Frisby. There was no way of knowing how long ago the Indian had left. Obviously, it was sometime before the shooting took place or the gunfire would have brought Tonto on the run.

"Watch tree mark," the note continued. Tonto, in following a trail that would be invisible to anyone else, had blazed the trunks of trees along the way so the Lone Ranger could come after him.

Then the Lone Ranger spoke. "Silver," he murmured confidingly to the big-muscled horse, "perhaps we're nearer the end of the chase than we thought. If Tonto's found a trail, and followed it, he did so because he felt it must be a pretty important thing to do. Otherwise he never would have left us." The Lone Ranger swung to the saddle and nudged his horse gently with an unspurred boot. He moved off in the darkness, feeling of the tree trunks as he went.

No one but Tonto could have hoped to follow such a trail as that made by the Night Legion when they went through the woods. In daylight, it would have been an almost impossible task, but at night, it was practically sheer instinct that guided the Indian friend of the Lone Ranger. Yet it was an unerring instinct.

As he went, Tonto held a heavy knife in his hand, and paused from time to time to cut an arrow-shaped notch in the bark of a cottonwood. When the trail turned one way or the other, he made a larger arrow, one that the Lone Ranger couldn't miss as he felt the trees in darkness. He made frequent stops to dismount and examine the ground by touch. The faintest of sounds of broken twigs, springing back to their original position, the soft depressions in the loamy ground, and even the scent of horses, served to assure him he was still on the trail of men who had recently passed. Tonto used four of his five senses in following that particular trail.

Then after what seemed hours, he came upon the camp quite suddenly. The outlaws were kindling a fire when he broke through the edge of a clearing, but they were so intent upon their work, they didn't notice him. Cautiously retracing his steps, he tethered his horse a safe distance away from the clearing, and returned on foot.

A Douglas Fir towered close to the edge of the camp of hooded men. Its broad, far-reaching branches formed a fragrant ceiling for a large part of the clearing.

Tonto glanced toward the men, and saw the fire beginning to take hold. They heaped more dry wood on the blaze. It was an eerie spectacle—a dozen men, each with a black hood covering his head and neck and falling in loose folds over his shoulders. Here was at least a part of the Night Legion. Tonto decided on a somewhat daring plan. Moving with the agility and grace of a cat, and equally as silent, he climbed the big evergreen, found a convenient branch from which he could see and not be seen, then settled himself to watch and to overhear whatever those men below might say.

So far, the hooded men had spoken only in low monosyllables, but when the fire was going good, they settled themselves around it and stuck out grimy hands to the warmth.

"Boss ain't come yet," one of them growled.

"Wal, we'll wait fer him. That's what he said to do."

"Why we gotta wait before we eat? Break out some grub an' let's stow it away. I'm famished."

"Shut up, Scar," advised another voice. "All you think about is eatin'."

Tonto made a mental note of the name Scar. Now, if they would only give the last name, it would be something to work on. The name of a member would be far more than all the previous efforts of the Lone Ranger and Tonto had been able to disclose about the Night Legion.

Scar spoke again.

"If the boss says anything about me bein' hungry, I'll ask him jest who it was that FOUND the old man's map."

"You found it all right, but it was jest pure luck."

"Yere? Wal call *this* luck, too." Scar held out a well-worn leather money belt. "I found this in that shack, too."

All the men showed interest.

"Mebbe yuh don't want tuh split up what's inside

it with me, bein as I found it, jest by *luck*. It's full of gold!"

"What'll the boss say?"

"He's said his say already. He said we could whack up the gold inside this belt amongst ourselves."

The men crowded close, eager for a share of the stolen gold, but the one called Scar, shoved the belt out of sight beneath his shirt. Tonto could almost see the self-satisfied grin he must be wearing beneath his mask. It was evident in his voice when he spoke again.

"I'm hungry, pards, an' when I'm hungry I don't feel much like dividin' up a lot of gold."

That put things in a new light for the men. Four of them moved at once, opening the saddle bags and bringing out supplies. Salt pork, coffee, hard tack, and the few utensils they used in cooking in the open were spread out near the fire. One of the men took a bucket to a near-by spring and returned with water. Tonto watched the proceedings with interest. He knew that to eat, the men would have to remove their black hoods, and this meant he'd have the chance to see their faces. He might recognize one of them.

The coffee pot was filled and balanced on rocks over the fire. One of the men opened a clasp knife and cut chunks from the pork.

Scar did nothing but watch. He probably felt he deserved waiting on, in view of the gold he was soon to pass out. Yet he had no reason to feel generous. He should have known these men who traveled with him.

Every one was a killer and none would hesitate to take his life for a share of the contents of the leather belt if he tried to hold out on them. They knew no law, save the one mysterious Boss who gave them orders.

Long minutes passed, and Tonto became cramped in one position, but he didn't dare to move to ease his aching muscles. The bacon was almost cooked, and the coffee pot was boiling. Now, at any instant, the meal might be declared ready. It was! Scar removed his mask! Tonto leaned forward slightly, to get a good look at his face.

The Scar for which he was named, was a livid crease from an old knife wound, starting at the chin and running up the left cheek until it was lost in the heavy tangle of coarse, black hair. His thick, shaggy eyebrows made his deep-set eyes seem even deeper. A cruel looking, thin-lipped mouth was surmounted by a broken nose that had healed with a twist to the left.

The other men, too, were now unhooded, and every one of them had a face equally sinister. Cruelty showed in every line. With one exception, the outlaws were clean-shaved. The exception wore a short-clipped beard. He was the man who spoke first after the meal began.

"Does any of you hombres know jest WHERE the Boss comes from?"

There was silence for a full half minute. The others looked at the speaker with surprise. Scar mouthed his food to one cheek and broke the silence in a slow voice.

"Anson, you bein' a new member of the outfit, have got a lot to learn. First an' most important thing is not to ask no questions."

"But ain't anyone ever seen the Boss? Don't none of you know who he is, or where he hangs out when he ain't with some of the boys?"

"Two men," replied Scar, "found out who he was. Jest two an' no more. Since that time, no one has been interested in findin' out. Jest take yer orders, carry 'em out, an' collect yer pay, an' let it go at that."

"What happened to the two that found out?"

Someone muttered, "Question-asking fool!"

Scar took a long swig from his tin coffee cup before he answered. "Both of 'em are dead. Some of the boys here seen 'em die, an' the way they suffered before they finally went out was horrible!"

Hardened men though they were, a couple of the outlaws shuddered visibly at the recollection of what must have been a frightful sight.

Scar tossed off the remainder of his coffee, then held the cup toward the squatting man nearest the fire for refilling. "Yuh see," he added, "the boss don't like his men tuh git too curious."

Anson nodded. "I savvy." For a moment he ate in silence, apparently considering what Scar said. Then he cleared his throat. "Gents, I suppose it's best not tuh be too curious, but they's one thing that's ranklin' in my mind."

All eyes turned toward him. A couple men muttered beneath their breath.

"Why'd the Boss stay behind instead of ridin' away from that shack with the rest of us?"

Several of the outlaws squirmed uneasily, another growled "blame curious fool won't last long in this outfit." The man known as Scar raked a thumbnail on his chin. It made a rasping sound against the bristle. He seemed to be something of a lieutenant to the unknown Boss. The others looked to him, waiting to see how he'd reply to Anson's latest query. Scar started to speak, then he changed his mind. His expression changed and a slightly amused look came into his face.

"Ain't you aimin' to answer a man?"

"Yeah, Anson. I'll answer yuh." Scar spoke in the tone of voice a man might use in speaking to a dull-witted child. "I'll answer you. Yuh see, the Boss don't like loose ends. When we finished up in the Frisby shack, he stayed around, tuh make sure there wasn't no loose ends that needed tyin' up. That's one of the reasons the Boss an' all the rest of us have kept clear of the law. He don't leave no loose ends danglin'."

As if that closed the subject, he rose to his feet, gulped down the second cup of black coffee, then rinsed his cup in a handy pail of water.

Tonto hugged close to the branch of the Douglas Fir. Even his Indian calm was shaken by the thought that any moment the boss of the Night Legion might be arriving to join the men in camp. The clump of a horse froze the outlaws to attention. Scar held his hand up, in a demand for silence, but the gesture was unnecessary. None of the outlaws moved or spoke.

There was no sound save the soft crackle of the burning fire. Each man reached for a gun, and waited, tense, ready for action. Then Scar relaxed. "It's all right boys," he said. "That's the Boss comin' here. I know his horse."

The Boss . . . THE BOSS of the Night Legion! Now, at last, after all these dragging months of trailing, Tonto was about to see the Boss!

CHAPTER V

The Fight

"Ho there!" The voice coming from the darkness of the woods outside the outlaws' camp had a
peculiar muffled quality, due perhaps to the heavy
black hood that enveloped the head and neck of the
speaker.

"Ho!" Scar shouted a reply. "That you, Boss?"

A coal-black mare entered the clearing in the woods.
The rider was a giant with huge barrel-shaped chest
and torso and shoulders of extreme breadth. Unlike
the other outlaws, this man wore a sombrero over the
black hood. "One of you take care of my hoss," he
ordered. Three men stepped forward, one held the
reins of the powerful animal, while another offered a
hand to aid the Boss in dismounting.

Disregarding the proffered hand, the Boss swung to
the ground. He moved with astonishing ease and agility for a man his size. Tonto, looking down from his
perch on the branch overhead, noticed that the boss
was shorter than he at first appeared. His legs were
unusually short for a man of his bulk. Had those
squat, slightly bowed legs been proportionate to his
torso, the man would have been at least eight inches
taller.

33

"How about some grub, Boss?" It was Scar who spoke.

"No!" snapped the leader. He walked close to the fire, then faced away from it, standing with his stubby legs slightly spread, his hands clasped behind his back. He studied each of the men around him, turning his hooded head slightly from one side to the other. Anson dropped his eyes, and fumbled with a bit of remaining food on his tin plate. The Boss seemed to stare at him. "New man?" he demanded, turning toward Scar.

"Yere, his name is Anson, Snake Anson. He's okay."

The hooded head nodded slightly. "Might bear a little investigation," he suggested. Another moment, during which the Boss eyed each one of his men through the eye slits of the mask. Then, apparently satisfied that all was as it should be, he began to speak in a less domineering style. "I was delayed some at the shack. There was a loose end that needed tyin'."

"That so, Boss?"

"Yere. A masked man came to the shack and doctored Frisby till he got the old galoot a-talkin'."

"Masked man?" Surprise showed in Scar's voice.

"*The* masked man, savvy?"

"Did yuh drill him?"

"No. I waited tuh see just how much Frisby could tell, then I seen he was tellin' more than he should, so I drew a bead on him through the window. I figured to get him first, then the masked man . . . but I missed."

"*You* missed?" Disbelief was evident in the voice

of the man who spoke. "Boss, you never miss."

"I did this time," snarled the leader. "The masked man saw a look in Frisby's face when the old galoot spotted me at the window. He whirled and fired just as I did. I got the old man, clean through the heart, but I missed the other. I had to hightail it " He paused and his men were silent. "Wal," he snapped, "I ain't the only one to miss my shot. The Lone Ranger missed the same as I did!"

Tonto's hand showed white across the knuckles from the way he'd gripped the branch in tension! Though the Indian had yet to kill his first man, and though he knew it was against the principles of the Lone Ranger, his companion, to shoot to kill even the most evil of outlaws, he had been ready to shoot the Boss, if his masked friend had been killed. Now, however, knowing that the Lone Ranger still lived, Tonto relaxed.

"You seem to have got away all right," suggested Scar.

"I got away all right, but I left a loose end. The same loose end that's pestered us fer months. Boys, the sooner we get that Lone Ranger, the better I'll like it."

The others nodded their agreement. "If," said Scar, "we don't get him, he'll sure as thunder get us."

"He might have got me tonight, if his horse hadn't been some distance from the shack."

"What's the plan now? Are we goin' to concentrate on gettin' the Lone Ranger, or go through with the other scheme?"

"Until I give you orders tuh the contrary, Scar, you'll go through with things jest as I planned 'em."

Scar agreed.

"We got the half o' the map now, an' that's what we went after. Now then, boys, here's orders. The westbound stage is due around the Gila Gap sometime tomorrow afternoon. There'll be two women aboard 'er. They're the nieces of Grant Whitcomb and they're goin' to the Whitcomb ranch tuh live there. They're due tuh leave the stage at Showdown an' go from there tuh the ranch by hossback."

"We're tuh stop the stage, an' stick it up, is that it?"

"That's right."

"What about the girls?"

"I don't want them hurt none. Rob the stage of all that's on't, then take all the girls have got, includin' the other half of the map that they'll have packed somewhere in their belongin's."

"What about the guard an' driver, d'ya want them tuh stay alive?"

"No use killin' 'em unless they happen tuh recognize some of yuh by yore voices. In that case, let 'em have some hot lead. The girls won't recognize yuh because they're strangers here. That's about all I got tuh tell you boys tuhnite. I'll leave yuh here now an' count on you gettin' t'other half of this map. When we git the hull of it, we'll have a gold mine all our own' an' a mighty good one too—one that ain't even been claimed or registered."

"Wait." Scar seemed to have sharper ears than the

others. He heard the faint sound that Tonto had heard a moment previously. The sound of a horse approaching. All the men grew tense. They were not expecting others of their gang. This new arrival could be no one but the Lone Ranger . . . the man whom above all others, they wanted to see dead.

The hoof beats stopped. Slowly, silently, every outlaw drew his gun, and moved slightly back from the fire. Anyone coming into the clearing would be attacked from all sides by a withering cross-fire that would cut him down almost instantly.

Then the soft call of a night bird floated on the air. Tonto heard it and knew it came from his masked friend.

"That," whispered the boss, "was a man-made call. Stand ready boys, it ain't none of our men."

The firelight's reflections danced on the cold steel of naked pistols. The almost inaudible snapping of gunhammers being drawn back struck Tonto with sinister meaning. He must act. He must in some way warn the Lone Ranger, or detract the attention of the killers. He decided and acted suddenly.

Tonto let out a piercing yell and dropped from his perch squarely on the back of the nearest outlaw. Even before his feet hit the ground as the outlaw went down, his hard-balled fist drove into the bristly bearded jaw with stunning force. The man grunted as a bone cracked, and went limp. But now the other men recovered from their surprise, a gun roared, lashing fire in a line toward Tonto. He felt the force of air as a slug whizzed past his head narrowly missing his left ear.

The outlaws had to hold their fire for fear of drilling some of their own number. They closed in on Tonto with fists and smashing gun butts. Tonto dove head on into the nearest of the men and heard a "whoosh" of air as he rammed the fellow's stomach. On his knees he caught himself, dodged out of the way as one of the killers kicked at him viciously and another came charging in. Blood covered the Indian's forearm where a stray bullet raked the flesh, but he felt no pain. He lunged at two of the men, grabbed each one in a brawny arm and brought their heads together. There was a cracking sound and both relaxed and slumped to the ground as the fighting redman dropped them and swung to ward off the crashing blow of a gun barrel swung with all the force of Scar's strong arm. It struck him a glancing blow that stunned him and brought blood spurting from his head. Mad rage in the Indian gave way to berserk strength. It was the Boss he wanted, the ruthless Boss of the Night Legion. His fighting fury brought him to his feet a dozen times when he went down. It sustained him . . . kept him fighting with the tenacity of a bulldog.

The fight went on with dazzling speed, only seconds had elapsed since Tonto dropped from the tree. Then a mighty shout rose above all the sounds of battle. A ringing cry rang through the camp. "Come on, Silver." Hoofs clattered close, pounding the ground

and the mightiest of all horses charged into the outlaws' midst. The Lone Ranger, a clubbed gun in each
hand, swung into the battle.

Scar leveled his gun pointblank, less than a yard from
Tonto's head. He fired and the gun jumped, belch-
ing orange flame, but the shot went harmlessly into
the air, for at the instant the outlaw squeezed the
trigger, the rearing forefeet of Silver lashed at him.
The killer went down, screaming and clawing in ag
ony. Again the white stallion rose high above the outlaws, lashing at them with his sharp, silver-shod hoofs.

"At them—at them, Silver old boy," encouraged the
masked man. To Tonto he yelled, "I've brought your
horse! Get to it! Get away, Tonto!"

He swung his guns viciously at the outlaws, fighting his way to Tonto's side. He seemed a part of the
mighty stallion, and the nimble Silver side-stepped,
plunged and kicked to keep the outlaws falling over
one another in their efforts to avoid being struck down.
Tonto was free for an instant.

"The leader got away," the masked man shouted.
"He's the one we want! These men don't count! Get
away while we're alive to go after the Boss!"

Tonto heard and understood. The odds against
them were too great for the fight to last long. It was
only because the outlaws were taken by surprise that
it had gone as long as it had. The men were already
regaining their feet, and bringing their guns to bear.
Another gun roared and the slug passed inches from
the masked man's head. He saw that Tonto was be-

side his own horse, leaping into the saddle, ready to ride. Then his voice lifted in a shout known through the length and breath of the entire region. "HEIGH YO, SILVER!"

The Night Legion screamed in rage. Their guns were blazing but their aim was hasty and hampered by the beating many of the men had taken. In their rage, the outlaws fired into the woods until their guns were empty, but they fired without a target, their bullets landing harmlessly among the trees, for the Lone Ranger and Tonto had escaped. Somewhere, beyond the circle of light in the clearing, the masked rider and the Indian were breaking through the woods. And Tonto had a lot to tell.

CHAPTER VI

The Stage to Showdown

Tonto threw more wood on the fire and with a crackling and sparkling the blaze curled up, fanned by the slight breeze that stirred through the cottonwoods. In the distance a pack of coyotes pierced the air with their cries.

After their escape from the camp of the Night Legion, the two had ridden for the better part of two hours to put plenty of distance between them and the outlaws. They were dog-tired from the many miles of riding since the afternoon of the day before. It must have been less than two hours to dawn when they finally felt it safe to stop, kindle as small a fire as possible, to ward off the chill of the pre-dawn period, and catch a little sleep.

But Tonto had a lot to tell, before the two could sleep. Lying near each other in their blankets, one listened while the other talked. The Lone Ranger found that Tonto already knew about the attack on old Joe Frisby, so he listened attentively while his friend related the outlaws' conversation.

Speaking in soft monosyllabic words, Tonto explained about Scar and Snake Anson; about the Boss who left no loose ends; and about the half-a-map that marked a gold mine. He told how the two girls, nieces of Grant Whitcomb were due that afternoon at Showdown, and how the outlaws planned to s op the stage and secure the other half of Joe Frisby's map.

At one point, the Lone Ranger interrupted. "As long as none of those men know who the Boss is, there's little to be gained by trying to capture them. The Boss is the man we want. The others are nothing but pawns, and he can replace them as fast as we can capture them. Furthermore, I don't think those we saw represent more than a tenth of the full membership of the Night Legion."

When the masked man finished speaking, Tonto asked, "You know about Whitcomb Ranch?"

"Not a great deal. I know it's a good-sized ranch about half a day's ride north of the stage trail between Gila Gap and Showdown. Whitcomb never married. He lives in the ranch house with an old Indian named Natacha who keeps house for him. He's been there for a long time." Tonto nodded slowly and the Lone Ranger continued. "Whitcomb has a lot of cattle and employs a lot of men to handle it. That's about all I know about him or his ranch."

Tonto knew much more than this, but he hesitated, wondering if it would be best to mention the weird things he had heard. The Lone Ranger might not know them, but there was a chance that the stories told by Indian friends of Tonto, brought from the ranch by old Natacha, were simply idle talk, without foundation of fact. There was one story about two men who went to the ranch and never returned. Little was said of those men, but it was generally known that theirs had been a one-way trail. They were definitely not among the men who worked for Whitcomb. There was another story, brought from the place by the aged Indian woman and circulated freely among the red men, but possibly unknown to the white folks. It dealt with the frantic screams, a man's screams of abject terror in the dead of night. Then silence, with no explanation for the screams.

Whitcomb himself was a peculiar sort of man. He rarely saw anyone save those who worked for him. He never came to town to mingle with the other ranchers of the region, never joined any of the ranchers' associations or attended any meetings. He seemed to live a life apart from his fellow men. Some bitterness in his past must have soured him on life in general. Not even his own men knew him well. All business connected with handling his ranch was left to his foreman who hired and fired the men and gave the orders, seemingly without interference or suggestion from the owner.

And there were other things. Most cowboys were prone to wander from one spread to another. They worked until the wanderlust got them, then pulled stakes and sought new berths. But not the men who worked for Whitcomb. He either paid them handsomely, or had some hold on them that made them stay year in and year out. Few men were hired to work there, and even fewer fired. A change in the staff of cattle handlers at the Whitcomb ranch was rare.

Tonto mulled all these things over in his mind. For some time after the steady breathing of the Lone Ranger showed him to be asleep, the Indian lay in his blankets, eyes closed, but wide-awake, trying to decide whether he should tell his friend all he knew of the Whitcomb place, or keep his knowledge to himself. Finally deciding on the latter course, he rolled in his blankets, settled himself, and slept.

The difference between the two girls who sat inside the lumbering stage heading for Showdown, was as great as the difference between night and day. Marge was slightly above the average height for a girl, slim, and somewhat stately in her bearing. Her hair was a deep chestnut, done in a soft coil low on her head. Of a serious nature, she rarely spoke, unless to make a soft-voiced statement of fact, or reply courteously to a question. Her younger sister Sally was short and agile, pert and blond. Sally's voice was high-pitched. She was inclined to prattle aimlessly, keeping up a running fire of talk about anything and everything that came into her head. Sally was a high-strung girl, filled with a joy of living, and thrilling to every new thing she saw on her great adventure.

The girls had never been West before this trip, and the thought of leaving their eastern home for good was somewhat appalling to Marge. She looked on the future in this wild and newly settled country with a feeling of uncertainty and bewilderment. Sally on the other hand, saw nothing to be afraid of. The vast stretches of open prairie, the mountains in the distance, and the occasional glimpse of cowboys in the towns the stage went through, thrilled every fibre of her being.

Sally was but eighteen, and Marge three years her senior. They were daughters of a pioneer who'd struck into the West when they were children. His wife had remained at home to care for the girls while their father tried to get his share of the good fortune that came to so many of the men who dared break into the new country.

Three years ago, Whitcomb returned east with good news, great hopes for the future, and half of a map showing where he and his partner had found their strike!

His plans had been to close all his affairs in the east, load his wife and daughters into a wagon and return to the rich, gold-bearing country to stake his claim with Joe Frisby. But his plans miscarried. First, he failed in his efforts to find backers for the venture. The mining of the gold would have to be hard-rock mining, which called for tools and supplies and these in turn required some cash.

Laughter and derision met all Whitcomb's efforts to sell an interest in his claim for the cash to work it. Then his wife died and this blow, on top of all his disappointment and discouragement, broke Whitcomb's health. In the year he lay bedridden, his meagre savings were used up. His house, mortgaged to the limit, went to the bank when he died, and Marge and Sally were left with nothing but half of a map, the word of their father that it was valuable, and a death-bed request that they write to his brother, telling full details of these past years, and ask him to provide a home for them.

The pride of the girls would have prevented their requesting Uncle Grant to house and feed them, but they were convinced that in the torn bit of paper, they had something of great value, and they were confident that with their uncle's aid they might locate Joe Frisby, secure the remainder of the map and find their inheritance.

Marge had the map securely pinned inside her shirt-waist. From time to time, while the stage bowled along the uneven trail, she felt to make sure it was still in place. Sally was half asleep in her corner of the big stage. She looked so like a child when she was asleep, Marge was amused. Then she turned to look at the passing landscape and made an alarming discovery.

Off to the north of the stage trail, and slightly in the rear of the big coach, a horse was running parallel to the stage. The horse was big and white, as fine a horse as Marge had ever seen. A lover of horses herself, the girl knew good horseflesh when she saw it, and despite the feeling of fear that sent a chill through her, she couldn't help but admire the easy stride and rippling muscles of the animal. But it was the rider that frightened her. His face was partly covered by a mask!

She had noticed the horse a mile back, but something else disturbed her attention before she saw the rider. Now she realized that the masked man was intentionally keeping pace with the stagecoach. Stories of murders and stagecoach robberies had been drilled into her by friends in the east who bade her farewell. Now all the things she'd heard came back to her. The guard and driver of the stage seemed not to have noticed the masked man who traveled with them.

Marge was not a coward or easily frightened by trifles, but here was grim reality. The rider was cutting in slightly, to lessen the distance between him and the stage. The guns he wore, were, to Marge, filled with menace. She nudged Sally with her elbow. "Sally, Sally, wake up."

"Huh? What's the matter?" Sally covered a sleepy yawn with her small hand, blinked her eyes at the bright sunlight that streamed through the windows of the stage, and sat erect. "What's the trouble," she demanded. "Have we reached Showdown?"

"No, but look over there." Sally looked where her sister pointed. "That man has been following us for some time, and I just noticed that he's masked!"

"Gosh," breathed Sally admiringly, "that's a fine horse, and he's sure a marvelous rider."

"But he's probably an outlaw! He's planning to rob the stage. He might kill us."

"Then we'd better be nice to him. I wonder Marge,"

went on the younger sister, "if he's as handsome as some of the men we've seen?"

"You're positively brazen."

"I'm darned near scared to death, but that won't help any. What do you suppose he'll do?"

"I—I wish I knew!"

The masked man was cutting in closer now, putting on a burst of speed to overtake and pass the stagecoach. Above the rattle of the stage and the clatter of the horses, his voice came to the girls. "Come on, Silver."

Marge put her head slightly out of the window to look at the trail ahead. She wondered if there were any sign of the town yet. The thing she saw made her more certain than ever that a holdup was at hand.

The trail led over a narrow bridge that spanned a creek. On each side of the trail, as it narrowed to meet the bridge, a dense tangle of weeds grew shoulder high. This, thought the girl, would furnish a hiding place for other highwaymen. The bridge itself was blocked by three horsemen. Even as she looked, Marge saw the men dismounting, leaving their horses to effectively close the bridge and stop the stage, while they came forward on foot with rifles held ready for use.

"Quickly, Sally," she ordered her sister, "get down on the floor where you'll not be shot."

"Not on your life," retorted the spirited Sally. "I'm going to stay where I can see what happens." Frightened though she might be, Sally was having the thrill of her life.

The driver's shouts were accompanied by a lurching of the stage and complaining creaks and squeaks of the springs.

They were stopping! The masked man on the white stallion came to a sliding halt close by them, holding two guns leveled at the guard and driver. An Indian and two more men appeared beside the stage on foot.

The girls had little to fear from thieves. Their supply of cash was pitifully meagre, and no one could possibly know about the torn bit of paper that Marge felt with her hand through the material of her waist. But possibly their uncle Grant was wealthy, the girls might be captured and held for ransom! All manner of awful things might be ahead.

The door of the stage was opened suddenly, and the dark face of the Indian appeared. Marge gave a frightened gasp of surprise. Sally stared at the level gaze that met her as Tonto looked inside. "Gosh . . ." she breathed, leaving the rest of her thought unspoken. Then Tonto commanded. "'You get-um out of there!"

CHAPTER VII

THE HOLDUP

"We—we'd better obey him, Sally," faltered Marge Whitcomb. "He looks frightfully dangerous."

Sally nodded her curly head and picked up the few belongings that had been inside the stagecoach with her. She looked beyond the brawny Indian, and thrilled inwardly at the sight of the tall, clean-cut looking man astride the powerful white horse. She saw his mouth and chin, beneath the black mask he wore, and frightened though she was, she wondered just how handsome the rest of the Lone Ranger's face might be.

Tonto stood slightly to one side to permit the girls to exit from the stage. One brown hand reached out to assist Marge in making the long step to the ground, but she ignored it, jumping lightly down. Sally was close behind her. Then for the first time the girls got a good look at the others. The guard sat with hands at shoulder level, and the driver was obeying emphatic commands from a grim-faced man on the other side of the stage. He tossed the girls' luggage from the top of the stage. It landed with a dull thud on the ground close by Sally.

"Why don't you two do something instead of taking their orders?" Sally's fear was outweighed by anger at the rough treatment accorded her few belongings. "What's the idea of not lifting a hand in defense of your passengers?"

The guard looked at the girl with an expression that was half annoyance, half amusement. "Better take it easy, Miss," he advised.

"Sure, you can take it easy. All you've got to do when these crooks are finished, is to drive on and tell how you've lost your passengers and luggage. What about us?"

"Sally!"

"Well, maybe you're willing to let these crooks get away with this, Marge Whitcomb, but I'm not." She stamped a small foot. "You . . . YOU," she shook her finger at the masked man. "You're the leader of these outlaws. You make them leave our things alone. There's nothing we have that's worth the stealing!"

"I'm sorry you think we're outlaws." There was something likable in the calm, courteous manner of the masked man. "But we're not. I can't take the time to explain things to the guard and driver, but I think one of my friends will assure them that they needn't worry about you."

"Not—not outlaws?"

"No. We came to meet you, to take you to your uncle's ranch. The men who brought those paint horses, will ride back to Showdown on the stage. The horses were brought here for you girls to ride."

"You, you're not going to rob us?"

The tall masked man shook his head.

"That's all the stuff they've got," called Buck Fisher, driver of the stage. "Everything has been explained, mister, so you needn't worry about the law bein' on yuh fer this affair."

"Very well," called back the masked man. "The men who helped me stop you are from the Sheriff's office. They'll go inside the stage, in place of the girls."

"Good."

"You might need their guns before you reach Showdown. You'll find they'll give a good account of themselves."

"Just who is this man?" demanded Sally of the grimfaced quiet guard who sat unmoved on the high seat. "If he isn't an outlaw, what's he wearing a mask for?"

"Jest do what he says an' you'll be safe ma'am." Jim Blunt took up the rifle he'd dropped when the other men showed gun muzzles. "Do what he says an' you'll be all right."

"That doesn't tell us who he is!"

"All I know is that he called his hoss Silver, an' there ain't no one knows his name." The guard spoke as if the very fact that the horse was named Silver was a guarantee of the masked man's character. Sally began to speak again, but a nudge from her sister changed her mind.

Tonto had already gathered all the bags and lashed them to the tie-strings behind his own and the Lone Ranger's saddles. Buck Fisher was gathering the reins to continue on the trail to Showdown and the guard's rifle was again cradled in his elbow. The two men who had apparently come from the Sheriff's office, if the statement of the Lone Ranger was to be believed, were climbing to the seat so recently occupied by the two girls.

"He speaks," whispered Marge, "as if he'd had some schooling. I don't know what there is about his voice, but—" she paused, and Sally took up where she left off.

"But you like him!"

"I feel that we can trust him!"

"I like him, too!" Sally had a way of interpreting her sister's statements as she wanted.

"Git up!" Buck Fisher cracked the whip and slapped the reins across the rearmost horses' flanks. Then, with a straining and a creaking, the stagecoach started on its lumbering way with the big iron-rimmed wheels churning clouds of hot dust from the trail.

"Now," said the Lone Ranger, "I can explain why we took this high-handed way of doing things."

Sally feigned a rage she didn't really feel. "It's about time you did some explaining. The very idea of stopping that stage, and ordering us about like this. And—and throwing our bags in the dirt. The very idea!"

"I'm sorry, but it was necessary."

"I don't see why! Uncle Grant wrote us and said there would be men to meet the stagecoach at Showdown! Instead of that, you—"

"Hush, Sally," admonished Marge.

"I'll do nothing of the sort," replied the smaller girl defiantly. She continued to berate the tall, masked man who secretly was pleased with her manner. He saw that all fear of him was gone. He saw, too, or rather some instinct seemed to tell him, that the girl was not really as angry as she appeared to be. When finally curly-headed Sally Whitcomb paused to take a much-needed breath, the masked man spoke.

"I'm really sorry we had to do it this way, but if we hadn't stopped you here, you would have been stopped just two miles beyond the bridge by real out-laws."

Marge paled at this. Her large eyes showed the fear that gripped her. "What . . . what," she stammered, "would outlaws want of us?"

The Lone Ranger felt that frankness would be best. "They wanted the map you brought here. Your father's map."

"B-b-but that . . . that map, I—I didn't think anyone knew!" Sally almost sputtered in her surprise at the calm statement of the Lone Ranger.

"I know about it, because I was with Joe Frisby when he died."

"Joe Frisby!"

"Yes." As briefly as possible the masked man related the essentials of Joe Frisby's murder and the stolen map. He told how he had gone to the Sheriff in the county seat and secured the aid of deputies. "They rode the horses Tonto and I borrowed for them, planning to go back on the stage."

The girls noticed the two horses, standing ready for their use.

"One of the outlaws has Joe Frisby's part of the map right now. When you two are safely at your uncle's ranch, we'll do what we can to recover that bit of paper."

"But how did you know we were coming here," asked Marge, still somewhat suspicious.

Skipping most of the details, the Lone Ranger explained how Tonto overheard the outlaws talking in their camp.

"Then," asked Sally, "how did these ou'laws know about the map?"

"I don't know. That's one of the things I hope to find out, and the sooner we get started for the ranch, the sooner I'll be able to devote my time to getting answers to a lot of questions."

Ma°ge nodded. Countless other questions raced through her confused mind. Things had happened so fast in the past half hour that she was hardly aware of what it was all about. One thing she *did* know. The precious bit of paper was still pinned securely to the inside of her clothing.

"I hope you can ride those horses, they were the most gentle ones we could find . . . in the time we had."

"Surest thing you know!" Sally's confidence had returned in full. "We rode a lot in the East."

Tonto's face, generally without expression, showed a trace of amusement at the girl. She would be due for some surprises if she thought the well-trained, mild-

mannered eastern horses were anything like the half-
wild, barely broken mustangs of the West. He moved
toward Marge to assist her in mounting.

The dark girl, however, hesitated. Her skirt was
undivided, and in no way suited for riding astride. The
saddle would never do for a long cross-country ride,
in the ladylike side-saddle form. She glanced at Sally
and saw her sister, unabashed, swinging her right leg
over the saddle with boyish ease, and ordering the
masked man to adjust the stirrups for her. Then blushing slightly, Marge also mounted.

The Lone Ranger seemed tense. From time to time,
throughout the entire talk, he had paused frequently
to listen. Then, as the two girls were finally ready for
the trip to Whitcomb's ranch, the faint sound of gunfire reached them. The worst fears of the Lone Ranger came to pass. Though the girls were safe, the outlaws had attacked the stage. They would be there in
numbers, to shoot it out with the guard and driver
and the two deputies.

He glanced toward Tonto, and saw the Indian shake
his head slowly in negation. The girls hadn't seemed
to hear the shooting.

The Lone Ranger had warned the deputies of what
might be in store, and they in turn had probably repeated full details to Buck Fisher and Jim Blunt. Fear
of battle, however, would never cause those men to
turn from the trail. They knew full well the ruthless
savagery of the Night Legion, and knew that when the
attack was made there would be no quarter given and

none asked. Yet, without hesitation, they'd gone on.

The attack had come with startling suddenness and no warning. It began when a fusillade of gunfire raked the stage, wounding both the guard and driver. The six big horses plunged and reared, clattering to a sudden stop as Buck yanked hard on the reins. The stabbing pain of a bullet in his shoulder added fury to his vicious handling of his six-in-hand. Jim Blunt was slumping on the seat, blood streaming from his temple. Buck grabbed the rifle, shouting to the men inside the stage, and leaped to the ground, firing as he dashed head down into a clump of trees from which the rifle fire had come!

"There they are," he yelled to the deputies who were scrambling from the stage. Each lawmen held a brace of guns, and all four guns were blasting hot lead at the outlaws.

Buck Fisher suddenly found himself surrounded by the killers. He swung the empty rifle at the nearest and it cracked against a man's hooded head. He heard one of the deputies behind him, gasp in pain. Throwing a quick glance in that direction, he saw the lawman falling to the ground with a red smear spreading across the front of his shirt and vest.

Cursing in justified rage, Buck fired the remaining bullets in his six-gun into those nearest him, and had the satisfaction of seeing two of the hooded men collapse. Then the hammer of his weapon fell on an empty chamber. There was no time to reload. Drawing back his arm, he flung the heavy gun with all his

strength, straight into the black hood of another killer. It hit hard, with a sickening thud, between the
eyeholes of the cloth. Then a thousand dazzling lights
seemed to burst in Buck Fisher's brain. A roaring filled his ears, and he felt himself slipping into a bottom-
less pit of total blackness.

When he recovered consciousness, he found himself sitting on the soft ground with his back propped
against a tree. His head ached frightfully, and his
shoulder throbbed where a bullet had drilled it. He
blinked his eyes, trying to clear away the fog from his
brain. When he tried to shake his head, the motion
sent new stabs of pain racing through his entire body.
Gradually the realization came to him, that he was
bound to the tree. Before him, half a dozen men were
lolling at their ease, with the hoods removed from ugly faces to make smoking possible.

Again he tried to shake away the clouds that ob-
scured his brain. The movement hurt. A thousand
pains shot both ways from his neck. Slowly, however,
Buck Fisher was able to take account of his surround-
ings. Jim Blunt was lashed to another tree near by.
Buck noticed the blood mixed with sweat and dust
that dried and caked on the guard's face. The Night
Legion hadn't bothered to treat Jim's wound. Buck's
shoulder had gone equally unattended.

Jim Blunt was conscious, but only barely so. His
lips were puffed and swollen, and a tiny trickle of
blood seeped from a corner of his mouth. His eyes
were glazed. There was an angry defiance that per-

sisted despite the partial loss of consciousness. The sight of his partner made Buck Fisher look away, but some awful fascination reclaimed his attention. One of the outlaws stood before Jim Blunt. His huge ham-like fists were clenched and his voice shook with rage.

"Talk, you close-mouthed son of a snake, or I'll let you have another in the same place." Jim Blunt tried to answer, but his battered lips could barely form words. The outlaw, however, must have understood the big guard's taunt. He swung his huge fist hard, and it smacked with a sickening thud against Jim Blunt's cruelly battered mouth. The blow, on top of all the others, was more than human flesh and blood could stand. Jim's head snapped back and merciful unconsciousness saved him further pain and torture for the time being.

"Now lookat what yuh done, Scar," one of the men growled. "Yuh went an' knocked him out before we learned where them two women went to."

"You mind yer own business, Anson," snarled Scar.

"I am," complained the other, "but now we gotta wait till t'other man comes to. Both them deputies are dead. If we're goin' tuh git any facts, we gotta git 'em from these two hombres."

Scar turned toward Buck Fisher when the man call-ed Anson spoke. His eyes lit with an evil satisfaction when he saw the young stagecoach driver conscious. "Wal!" he drawled in satisfaction. "It looks like we don't have no waitin' at all."

Scar walked slowly toward Buck Fisher, massaging

his knuckles as he did so. "We aim to find out where yore passengers went to. They was supposed tuh be on that stage till it got tuh Showdown, but they wasn't on board. Now if you know what's smart, you'll save me a lot o' trouble, an' yerself a lot o' misery, by talkin'!"

Buck was trying hard to think! Refusal would bring the same treatment Jim Blunt had received. He glanced toward the sun, carefully calculating the time he must have been unconscious. It was much lower in the sky than when he'd first stopped the stage at the Lone Ranger's command.

By this time the two girls would be almost to the Whitcomb ranch. It would be too late for the hooded men to overtake them, even if the killers knew where they had gone. Moreover, the sisters were in the care of the Lone Ranger. Surely, between the Lone Ranger and Grant Whitcomb, with all his cowboys, the girls would be quite safe. "All right," Buck Fisher said, "I'll talk."

Scar grinned. "That's good sense."

"Easier than I thought it'd be," commented Anson, and a couple of the other men nodded their heads in satisfaction.

"Go on," commanded Scar. "Where's the girls gone?"

"How do I know you'll let me go, if I tell you," countered Buck Fisher.

"Yuh don't."

"Then what's there for me to gain by talkin'?"

"You've seen what yer guard got fer *not* talkin'."

"Sure, but how do I know I won't get the same, after I'm done tellin' you all I know about the girls?" Buck was stalling for every possible moment. The more time he could allow the girls and their escorts the greater their margin of safety.

Scar tugged at his heavy gun belt, and hitched up his greasy trousers before he replied. "See here, driver, it's up to the Boss what happens to you. *Don't* talk, an' you git rough handlin'. Talk, an' we take yuh tuh the Boss an' he's the one decides what happens."

"He ain't goin' to let me go free, after I've seen the faces of you men."

"They's several ways a man can die. Some of them ways," Scar paused to emphasize his statement, "some of them ways are awful hard."

"I savvy."

"I'm gettin' mighty tired of waitin' fer you to start tellin' things."

"The girls are where you can't get to 'em. They left the stage a good ways back where they met a couple men with extra hosses, an' rid overland to the Whitcomb ranch. Does that answer your questions?"

"Ain't they goin' to Showdown at all?"

"No they ain't."

"I wondered if that confounded redskin heard the plans." It was Snake Anson who spoke.

Scar glanced at Anson.

"The redskin that jumped us from that fir tree last night," explained Anson. "He must've been hid there

durin' the time the Boss outlined this affair." He flip-
ped his half-smoked cigarette away from him, then
asked, "Was it a masked man and an Injun that took
them girls from the stage?"

Buck didn't try to suppress the grin he felt. "It sure
as thunder was," he stated. "What's more, that masked man is known pretty generally as the Lone Ranger."

Scar cursed at the news. "He's interferin' too blame
much in what we do! That's twice that hombre's
crossed our trail an' made us come out second best."
He finished with vile curses, then stepped forward and
with his open hand slapped Buck Fisher on the side of
his head with a force that made the driver dizzy. "The
Boss has gotta know this," he shouted to his men. "I
better ride right away an' tell him."

The men nodded agreement.

"I'll get started pronto an' leave a message in the
hollow tree where he c'n find it. You Snake Anson,
take charge of these two survivors."

"Me?" There was surprise in Anson's voice. "I'm
sort of new in the organization to be takin' charge of
things."

"I says for you tuh take charge an' that settles it."

"But what's that same include? What'm I tuh do
with these two? Fix their wounds an' coddle 'em like
a nursemaid?"

"No," bellowed the infuriated Scar. "Take charge
of fixin' em so they can't tell anyone who they seen in
this outfit. You know what the Boss says. *Don't leave
no loose ends.*"

"Oh." Anson apparently understood and, with a sinking of all his hopes, Buck Fisher likewise understood. Scar had pronounced the penalty of death. He would leave Anson to carry out the details.

Buck watched Scar as he swung into the saddle of an awaiting horse. In every move the outlaw made, there was a vicious ruthlessness. He jerked the horse's head around in a manner that made Buck Fisher, a lover of good horseflesh, writhe in rage. He jabbed his three-inch rowels into the tender flesh of the horse's side, and rode away.

Then Snake Anson rose to his feet. "Boys," he drawled, taking his gun from its holster with meticulous care and examining its chambers, "I reckon I'm the one selected fer tyin' up loose ends, because they might be some doubt as tuh the stuff I'm made of. Chicken-hearted, white-livered man ain't no place in the Night Legion. It looks like I've been called on tuh prove I ain't none o' them things."

The others watched Snake Anson with keen interest. They, too, knew Scar had appointed him executioner to test him, and they wondered if he'd falter in his task or go through as ordered.

"I wonder," said Snake Anson, "jest what you boys would do if I was tuh refuse tuh carry out Scar's orders?" He glanced around him, and saw several men reach slowly for their six-guns. He chuckled softly, "That's what I thought. Was I to refuse, there'd be three shootin's takin' place here instead of only two. Wal I ain't aimin' tuh refuse."

The killer was calm and deliberate as he carefully examined his heavy gun. He knew all eyes were on him, and he seemed to enjoy his temporary prominence.

Buck Fisher glanced at Jim Blunt. "Glad poor Jim's unconscious," he thought. "He won't never know what hit him."

Finally Snake Anson closed his weapon with a snap and walked toward Jim Blunt.

A moment later the air was shattered by the thunder of a heavy gun in Anson's hand. Then a second blast close on the heels of the first. A killer had proved himself a true member of the Night Legion.

CHAPTER VIII

THE HOODOO RANCH

It was dusk when the Lone Ranger, Tonto, and the two girls came within sight of the Whitcomb ranch. Throughout the entire ride, the masked man had said little. His replies to many questions of the girls were short, and after several attempts to engage him in conversation, both Marge and Sally gave up in despair.

His mind was filled with bitterness. The shooting he heard when the long ride was just about to begin could have but one meaning. The Night Legion killers had met the stage. Such a meeting could have but one outcome. The lawmen, guard and driver would give a stiff fight, but the odds would be too great, especially with the outlaws firing from ambush. Though there could have been no other way, the Lone Ranger felt responsible for sending four men to their deaths. It sickened him, and yet, it was a case of the men or the girls. True, the Boss had given orders that the Whitcomb girls were to go unharmed, but with men the type of those seen in the clearing and girls like Marge and Sally, there was no assurance that the orders of the Boss would be obeyed in their entirety.

The Boss was primarily interested in securing the girls' part of the map. His interest in the welfare of the girls was secondary. Who was this mysterious Boss? Not even his own men seemed to know him, yet he had some hold on them that made them follow out his every order—carry out his every plan for robbery and murder. Where did the Boss meet the men to give them orders? How many members had this powerful Night Legion? Surely there were others than those seen last night in the woods. There had been times, when large herds of cattle were stolen, and at least three score of the hooded men had ridden at one time.

Where was their headquarters? Where had Scar and Anson come from? Though the Lone Ranger knew the West better than most men, he'd never heard of either of the two before last night. But there was no use guessing. As soon as the girls were safe in the care of Grant Whitcomb, he and Tonto would return to the clearing in the woods. There might be clues there that would furnish at least a starting point in the long drawn out hunt for the mysterious Boss of the Night Legion! After all, more had been learned in the past twenty-four hours, than previous months had taught him.

The Lone Ranger snapped from his reverie when Sally jabbed him in the side with a tiny fist. "I've had about enough of this silence-you-can-cut-with-a-knife," she said. "We're almost at the ranch, if that's it ahead of us, and I'd like to know something about who you are."

"That isn't at all important."

"Why are you so interested in helping us? Are you on Uncle Grant's payroll?"

"No."

"Did he send you to meet the stage? Does he know you?"

"I don't think he ever heard of me."

"Then why—"

"Sally," interrupted Marge, "if he doesn't want to talk, don't ask so many questions. After all, he has been very kind to help us as he's done."

"It doesn't strike me as kind to make one so curious," Sally was riding beside the Lone Ranger, with Marge and Tonto in the rear. "There's one thing you might tell me, even if you won't tell anything else."

"Yes?"

"Where'd these horses come from?"

"They were borrowed."

"From whom?"

"Your uncle. We are going to leave you in a moment, and you'll finish the ride alone. When you get to the ranch, simply turn the horses loose in the corral, and they will have been returned. Your uncle might be somewhat worried about them. He doesn't know we have them."

"I wonder," interrupted Marge, "what Uncle Grant will have to say about this cross-country ride. I'll wager he'll be furious to hear that there was a plan to rob us."

"He'll be mad enough to chew nails!" A little look

of perplexity brought tiny wrinkles to Sally Whitcomb's forehead. "I wonder, Marge, what Uncle Grant
is like!"

"So do I."

"Have you never seen him?" asked the Lone Ranger.

Sally answered, "Never." Then she went on,
"There is a reason why I'd like to get you talking. I've
heard a few things about Uncle Grant's place."

"Have you?"

"Yes I—we have. When we were changing stages
back at Eagle Pass a station agent asked where we were
going and I told him. What do you think he said?"

Tonto leaned forward eagerly in his saddle. Though
the masked man would possibly know nothing about
the strange things that were said to have transpired
at the Whitcomb Ranch, the Indian had heard innumerable stories.

"He told us," went on Sally, "that it was a Hoodoo
Ranch."

The Lone Ranger looked curiously at the girl. His
mouth moved slightly as if in amusement. He was
familiar with the methods of "kidding" employed by
practical jokers in the western communities and at-
tributed the story told the girl to one of these.

Tonto on the other hand, became more grim than
ever.

"What do you suppose that man meant by telling
us that sort of thing?"

"I'm sure," replied the Lone Ranger, "if there is
anything about your uncle's ranch that you should

know, he himself will tell you. You'll be there in a few minutes more." He reined in and signalled the others to bring their horses to a halt. "Here," he said, "is where we leave you."

"I don't see why! Come on along with us, and meet our uncle," invited Sally Whitcomb.

The masked man shook his head. "I'm afraid he would wonder why I didn't remove my mask. You'll have no trouble now."

But Sally was not so easily convinced that the time for parting had arrived. She wanted desperately to break through the shell of reserve and find out more about the mysterious rider who had so little to say, and who always kept his face concealed. At first she coaxed and pleaded, then she demanded. Even the reserved Marge extended a most cordial invitation to go on to the ranch with them, and stay for supper. But the Lone Ranger and Tonto were anxious to be away. They wanted to get back to the woods, to look around the clearing where the outlaws met last night. Tonto had already transferred the girls' bags to their own horses.

"Well, anyway," finished Sally in desperation, "when you're around this way, stop in. We'll always be glad to see you." She stuck out her hand and gripped that of the Lone Ranger in a firm, boyish handclasp.

"We truly will," added Marge. "And thanks for all you've done."

"You're more than welcome." Then the masked man and the Indian swung their horses and rode off without a backward glance. For a long moment, the two girls watched the retreating stallions. There was a strangely soft light glowing in the dark eyes of Marge Whitcomb. Sally sighed deeply. Then the girls, too, rode on. Ahead, the buildings of the Whitcomb ranch marked the end of their long journey from the East. The place looked quite commonplace. Surely there was nothing in the general appearance to indicate the dreadful things that lay in wait there for the newcomers. If the girls had only known . . . . they would have understood why their uncle's place was called a "Hoodoo Ranch."

The horses paused of their own volition when they reached the corral. Marge and Sally swung stiff-legged to the ground. They were more cramped and lame than they expected to be from the long ride on the western horses, but they were glad to be here. "At last," breathed Sally, "we're someplace that we can call home, where there won't be such worries about money." She yawned and stretched her arms, then tried a couple of steps. "Ohhh gosh," she groaned, making a wry face, "I'll never be able to walk tomorrow. My legs are tied in knots!"

Marge, more sensitive than Sally, possibly more receptive to impressions, felt a vague uneasiness. There was something about the place that made her apprehensive. She looked about on all sides. There was the corral, with a good stock of horses, just as one might expect to see on any well-kept ranch. The fences and buildings, as far as she could see, were in good repair.

In the distance a few cows grazed contentedly. Everything was as it should be and yet there was something queer.

"A fine reception," complained Sally suddenly. "The least he might do is to have someone help us with our luggage." She was fumbling with the knots of the tie strings, loosening the bags so recently put there by Tonto.

"That's it!" burst out Marge.

"Huh?"

"Oh, I—" hesitated the older girl, "I was wondering what there was about this place that seemed so strange. There's no one around."

"That's so." Sally looked toward the bunkhouse, which was dark inside. "There should be a lot of cowboys around here someplace. Maybe they're out on the range, or—" she recalled some of the terms she'd heard, "or maybe they're lineriding."

Marge hoped some simple explanation would solve the riddle, but she felt inwardly that there was something more than that. Sally shrugged her shoulders, tossing off worry easily. "Just means we've got to lug our own bags in, that's all." She took one in each hand, "You take the others, Marge," and started toward the rambling comfortable-appearing house.

Marge picked up the other bags and followed, envying her sister's nonchalant ease in almost any situation. There were times when Sally reminded her of an impetuous young colt; carefree, unrestrained, agile, and brimming over with a healthy joy of living.

The bags plunked to the porch floor and Sally rapped on the door. A moment's wait brought no response and she tried again, harder this time than before. More waiting, and still no sign of life from within the house. "Funny," she muttered, "Uncle Grant knew we'd be here sometime today." She hammered on the door with both fists and under the force of the blows the door creaked slowly inward. "It's unlatched!" she observed.

Pushing it wide, Sally took up the bags and boldly walked inside. Marge followed closely, with her uneasiness increasing many fold. Outside, it was dusk, but no lamps had been lighted in the room. The girls stood still a moment, just inside the door, trying to accustom their eyes to the darkness.

The first impression of the room was its vast size. Compared to the small "parlors" the girls knew in the East, the living room of the ranch house was a vast expanse of space. As they took in more of the details the girls saw rugs of Indian weaving on the floor, and others hanging decoratively on the wall. Directly opposite the outside door, there was an entrance to a hallway that seemed to run straight back into the other part of the house. A massive table stood against the wall on each side of the arched door leading to the corridor, and over one table a gunrack hung suspended from the wall, while a big elk's head overhung the other.

Windows facing toward the south filled the wall on the girl's right side, and a huge fireplace was at the opposite end of the room. The fireplace intrigued Marge and Sally. It might have been a cheerful sight with a warm fire of pine logs blazing and crackling, but in the dim light the gray stones looked cold and forbidding to the touch. Then Marge gasped with a quick intake of breath. For the first time she saw the figure next to the fireplace.

The man sat in a heavy chair with a blanket across his lap, falling over his knees. He was a heavy man, almost filling the big chair, but the impressive thing —the thing that gave him an almost repulsive appearance was his head. It was white, and perfectly round, without a trace of hair. Small piglike eyes of pale blue color watched every movement of the girls. His small short nose and pinched mouth were far too small for the rest of him. Small ears were flat against his head. He seemed waiting for one of the girls to speak.

CHAPTER IX

THE IRON RING

The bald-headed man seemed quite willing to wait indefinitely for one of the girls to break the long silence. Sally was the first to recover her composure after the first shock of surprise at seeing the one who obviously was her uncle, sitting there without a word of any sort in the way of greeting or welcome.

"I—I suppose," she said hesitantly, "you are our uncle, Grant Whitcomb?"

The silent man nodded without speaking.

"We—er—uh—we are the daughters of your brother. Y—You wrote to us . . . you told us it would be all right to come here to live with you."

Again Grant Whitcomb nodded

"Well . . we . . we're here!" Sally laughed nervously to cover her confusion. "We're here, and I suppose you wonder who is who. That . . . that is Marge, I'm Sally."

Marge finally broke into a one-sided conversation. "If you are Uncle Grant, you know why we came here. I—I do hope it isn't going to be too much of an inconvenience to have us here. We have hopes of finding father's claim. In that case, we'll be able to support ourselves." She was bewildered by his attitude.

For the first time, Grant Whitcomb spoke. "Did you," he said in a voice that was emotionless, slightly high-pitched, and certainly not cordial, "bring the map with you?"

At any other time, Marge might have thought it odd that he'd speak first of all about the map, with no inquiry concerning the long trip West, but now she was too much shaken by the many exciting events that had crowded themselves into one day of a heretofore uneventful life to think much of anything. She merely nodded that she had the map.

"Have any trouble on the trip?"

"Yes!" Sally picked up the conversation. "Someone knew we had that map and planned to steal it from us. We were met before we got to Showdown by some men who supplied horses. We rode overland to get here."

A look of interest crossed Grant Whitcomb's face, but it was just a fleeting change of expression that passed quickly. His eyes widened slightly and had there been eyebrows, they would have lifted in a questioning invitation to supply more details.

"One of the men was an Indian, the other wore a mask."

"Rot!"

Sally repeated his comment questioningly. "Rot?"

"What do you mean?" asked Marge.

"How could anyone know you had that map? D'you

expect me to believe that sort of story, just because yer late gettin' here?"

Sally's face burned red with anger at the accusation. "We were told about the map by the masked man, and he knew about it because he was with Joe Frisby when he died."

Whitcomb squinted slightly. "With Frisby when he died. So he's dead, eh?"

"Yes, and what's more he was murdered by the men who stole his part of the map. I guess we told you all about him when we wrote you."

"Yuh mentioned Frisby, yeah."

Sally still fumed with rage at the man's manner. "What's more, the only one who knew about that map was you! It's through your telling of it that these outlaws killed Joe Frisby."

"Sally," admonished Marge, "you mustn't speak like that."

"Well, he needn't accuse us of fibbing to him then!"

"How do you know," asked Whitcomb slowly, "that the masked man you tell about, ain't the one that murdered the old man?"

This thought hadn't occurred to either of the sisters. Something about the Lone Ranger made them feel he wasn't a man who would commit a murder. Yet, all things considered, their uncle's idea might be right. Certainly the man had kept his face concealed, and he *had* acted very strangely.

"Perhaps," continued Grant Whitcomb, "he wanted to make sure you had the map with you. It's my bet we haven't heard the last of him. Like as not, he'll come snoopin' and prowlin' around my house, makin' no end of trouble, tryin' to get the rest of the map from you!"

"But he had many chances, if that's what he wanted," countered Marge. "He could have demanded it any time he wanted to and we'd have had to give it up."

"We haven't heard the last of him," insisted the bald-headed man. "But we'll handle him if he comes this way." He clapped his hands. "Natacha, that's the old Indian housekeeper, will show you where you're to sleep."

Sally felt that she'd never learn to like the man who faced her, but she hoped he'd turn out differently than the first impression indicated. He spoke again.

"Natacha!" Whitcomb looked beyond the girls. They turned and saw the Indian standing in the hallway. "Show my nieces to their room." To the girls he said, "We'll have a talk later on." His tone seemed a dismissal for the night. He had made no apologies for his manner of receiving them, no explanation for remaining in his chair without rising, and no offer of food or invitation to refresh themselves and then return to the big living room for conversation.

In one hand, that resembled more than anything else the claws and talons of a bird of prey, Natacha held an oil lamp. With the other hand, she beckoned for the girls to follow her. By the light of the lamp, they saw her face. It was a mass of seams and wrinkles.

Neither girl had ever seen a face to equal it. The skin seemed to hang in loose folds overlapping one another. Straight black hair done in two braids bound with dirty red ribbon, came from the back of her head to fall over each shoulder almost to her hips. Her lean, narrow shoulders slanted to wide hips from which fell voluminous folds of a varicolored skirt that must have had a lifetime's accumulation of filth on it. She slumped rather than walked, her moccasined feet making a sort of sliding sound on the pine flooring.

Silently the two girls followed Natacha, carrying their luggage. "I'm starving," muttered Sally. "I wonder if there isn't a chance of getting a bite to eat?"

"Uncle Grant didn't suggest it, Sally."

"Well, I'm suggesting it! He probably thinks we've eaten."

"Where would we have eaten? We've been in the saddle since early afternoon."

"Perhaps Natacha can help, if . . . " Sally paused, "if she can talk enough English to understand us." Raising her voice a trifle, she addressed the aged woman. "Natacha."

Natacha paused before a door, turned half toward Sally and looked at the girl.

"Do you speak English?"

Natacha nodded vigorously. "Me Sabe!" She pushed the door open and went into what proved to be a comfortable-looking bedroom. Placing the lamp on a small stand, Natacha stood aside to make way for the girls to enter.

Of medium size, the bedroom was meticulously clean. A big double bed in one corner showed clean, white sheets folded back beneath huge downy-looking pillows. In case the night turned chilly, there were blankets folded at the foot. An oval hooked rug covered almost all of the floor beside the bed. Two upholstered chairs flanked the washstand above which hung huge, fleecy towels. One wall supported a long shelf, slightly over head-high, with a row of pegs beneath it to hold clothing. Sally opened the top drawer of the heavy dresser, ran her finger across the bottom, and then scrutinized the digit close to the light. "Nice and clean," she said approvingly, looking toward Natacha. The old woman grinned toothlessly in response.

Encouraged by what probably was meant for a smile, Sally pressed Natacha for something to eat. "Bimeby," was the croaked response. Natacha left, closing the door behind her.

"Bye and bye," sighed Sally, "that might mean some time tomorrow."

"Let us hope not." Marge sat on the edge of the bed then fell back with a deep sigh. The day had been a cruelly hard one for girls not used to the rigors of life in the West. Marge was desperately tired and her slender body seemed a mass of aches and pains from riding.

Sally tossed her coat on the nearest chair and tugged at her shirtwaist. "First of all," she decided, "I'm going to wash up, and then I'm going to see about the food situation." She poured water from the pitcher into the basin, and in a moment was sputtering with energy, dousing her face with cold water. It freshened her a lot.

Marge, watching from the bed, mused at the way Sally, in times like this, seemed so much more capable and self-sufficient. "I wish," she murmured, "I had some of your energy and spunk."

"Well, we're here, and we're here to stay, so we may as well make the best of it."

"What do you think of our uncle?"

"Haven't decided yet," was the matter-of-fact reply. "Tell you better when I've seen more of him." She opened one of the bags and from the depths extracted a comb. Standing before the mirror on the back of the door, she ran the comb through her tangled hair, chattering about her hunger. "If we don't hear about some food when I get finished, I'm going out to find the pantry or the larder or whatever they call it, and help myself!"

Marge drew herself to sitting, then bent to unlace her high boots to change to something more comfortable. A slight crinkle beneath her blouse reminded her of something. "The map! Sally, we must do something with it. Hide it."

Sally tossed the comb in the general direction of the dresser, missed the mark and saw the comb clatter to the floor.

She retrieved it, and put it on the dresser. "Get the map, I'll find a place to hide it." She looked about the room, stroking her chin with a forefinger, a habit of hers when she pondered seriously. "I know," she said. "Beneath the rug."

Marge was too tired to argue, knowing full well that Sally would cry down any other suggestion. The rug would be as good a place as any, at least, for the time being. They could discuss the matter with their uncle later on. Yet would they? Marge recalled how Uncle Grant asked first of all about the map. Was he a man who could be trusted? She tried to tell herself he was. Surely the brother of her father would be loyal. Yet there was a lot about Grant Whitcomb that somehow didn't ring quite true. Now if it were the stranger with the mask . . . "Strange," she thought. "He was masked, he didn't tell us who he was, he didn't do a thing to make us feel he could be trusted, and yet he seemed so much more so than our uncle."

"Where is it?" demanded Sally.

Marge passed the small bit of paper to her sister, who kicked back one end of the oval rug. Both girls noticed the iron ring sunk into the floor. It was characteristic of them that Marge asked, "What's that?" at the same moment Sally dropped to her knees to investigate and find out for herself.

Sally lifted on the ring and it swung upward to furnish a handgrip. There was a square section in the floor that probably lifted up to give access to what was underneath. "That looks interesting," murmured Sally. She tugged on the ring, but nothing happened.

"Perhaps Uncle Grant wouldn't want us to poke into things Sally."

"Don't be so darned bashful."

"But after all, it isn't our home."

"It's going to be the only home we'll have. We may as well know something about it," Sally grunted as she put all her strength into lifting. "I can't budge this thing, come here and give me a hand."

Marge hesitated. "Let's get cleaned-up first, there will be lots of time to see what's down below."

"Probably nothing but a cellar anyway." Sally dropped the map on top of the trap door, replaced the rug, and began to open the remaining bags to find fresh clothing. Then a rap sounded on the door.

"Oh," breathed Sally. "Perhaps that's old Natacha with a lunch."

"Girls." Grant Whitcomb's voice called outside the door.

Marge replied, "Yes?"

"You comin' out soon?"

The girls exchanged quick glances. Sally grinned and whispered, "Maybe he's going to be sociable after all." Aloud she said, "We're cleaning up, be out in fifteen minutes."

"Very well, but be as quick as you can. Supper's on the table and it won't stay hot for long." His footsteps sounded as he moved away.

Sally flung her hand above her head and made a silent gesture of glee. "Hurray," she whispered, "we eat."

Marge wondered if she hadn't judged her uncle too hurriedly, and determined to try to like Grant Whitcomb till she had definite reason to feel otherwise.

Sally's hands were flying as she piled clothing on the bed, unpacking the four bags. "Hurry up, Marge, the sooner you're dressed, the sooner we eat. *And,*" she added, "the sooner we'll know more about our uncle!"

CHAPTER X

THE RETURN OF THE MASKED MAN

Whatever Natacha might lack in youth and beauty, she more than made up in her skill as a cook. Hot biscuits, fried spring chicken, with lots of tasty gravy, and an almost endless assortment of vegetables and fruits made Sally Whitcomb glad that she'd been hungry. She continued eating long after her uncle and sister were finished, wondering how so grand a meal could be prepared on such short notice. She reasoned that her uncle, anticipating the arrival of the girls, had given orders for a special dinner with instructions to have everything ready for the girls as soon as they came. Brought up in an eastern city where food was bought and prepared in small quantities for economic reasons, she was unused to the wholesale western way of doing things.

Even Marge, apprehensive as she was, forgot her vague worries during the course of the meal. Natacha refilled the girls' milk glasses and Grant Whitcomb poured himself a second cup of coffee then stoked a big foul-smelling pipe and leaned back in his chair. From time to time he'd asked short questions about the trip, but now he seemed ready to go into a more lengthy conversation. "Had quite a trip then, didn't yuh?" he inquired of Marge.

"Yes indeed! We've never ridden so far on horse-back."

"You won't get the chance to do much ridin' here for quite a spell."

"Why is that? The horse we rode seemed quite gentle, almost as gentle as the eastern riding academy horses."

"Havin' outlaw trouble around here. That's why."

"We heard something about that," interrupted Sally. "Something about the Night Legion, isn't it?"

Grant Whitcomb frowned and sucked in silence on his pipe. He blew a billowing cloud of smoke toward the ceiling, cursed softly beneath his breath and finished with—"Night Legion is right! If them thievin', murderin' polecats ain't caught up with plenty soon, there won't be a ranch this side of the Mississippi that'll be makin' money."

"We haven't heard a great deal about the Night Legion."

"Well, they's aplenty tuh tell. They don't stop at nothin'! Rustlin', hoss-stealin', robbery, torture, murder an' all the rest!" He went on to give a lurid account of some of the atrocities of the Night Legion. Things that made Marge pale and left even Sally momentarily speechless. "And that masked man," he finished, "was like as not the leader!"

"I don't believe it!"

Grant Whitcomb glared momentarily at Sally who

dared make such a frank, outspoken statement. Sally, unabashed, returned the steady gaze.

"And," said the man slowly, "why don't you believe it?"

"Because I like the way he talked!"

"Humph!" snorted the bald-headed man, "as if you could tell anything about a man by the way he talked! You'll learn, before yer here fer very long, that the slickest crooks are likewise the slickest talkers, an' the boss of this Night Legion is about the slickest crook that ever drawed a breath!" He paused to puff deeply on the pipe, and then went on. "What's more, your tellin' him you had that map he's after, will likely make no end of trouble for me! He'll come pussyfootin' around here tryin' to git it, an' likely drill some of my men."

In an attempt to change the subject before the fiery Sally spoke again, Marge broke in. "Is that why you said we couldn't do much riding while we're here?"

"You girls ain't to leave the house until I say so!"

"C-can't leave the house," repeated Sally. "What are we going to do in the house all the time?"

"You'll have to do somethin' to pass the time. Maybe when the boys are around, you c'n go as far as the corral, an' mebbe, when they's guards to ride with you, you can take a little canter on the range, but you ain't to go nowhere's without my sayin' so, an' that's final."

The man reverted to his curt manner again, after thawing out slightly during the meal. Marge glanced at her sister, and saw the girl about to express an opinion that might lead to further words. She broke in hurriedly, "Uncle Grant."

"Wal?"

"Where are all the men? I thought they'd be around the corral some place. We haven't seen a sign of anyone but you and Natacha."

"Men are busy," was the short and uninformative response.

Sally compressed her small, pert mouth, and kept her eyes down on her plate. Marge felt that this was the beginning of a feud between the high-strung girl and Grant Whitcomb. Sally was not a girl to take such unreasonable orders from anyone, least of all a man who had acted with as little cordiality as their uncle.

Whitcomb seemed to be struggling with himself. He kept his face buried in a cloud of smoke, and several times began to speak, but each time stopped himself. When finally he did speak, he was again the mild-mannered individual he'd been before the flare-up started with the talk of the Night Legion. "By the way, Margy, you said something about that map being with you."

Marge nodded her head.

"Where is it now? Maybe I'd better put it in safe keepin' till the law rounds up the Boss of the Night Legion."

Marge was about to tell her uncle that the map was concealed beneath the oval hooked rug, but before she could speak, Sally answered for her. "We haven't found it yet."

"Haven't found it?"

"Nope," she fibbed. "It's packed with our clothes somewhere, but we haven't had the chance to unpack all the bags."

"Don't tell me you've lost it," barked Grant Whitcomb.

"Oh, it isn't really lost, it's somewhere among our things. It'll turn up sooner or later."

"You don't seem much concerned about it." There was a ring of suspicion in the man's voice.

"I'm not, that is, we're not, because we know we put it in one of the bags. We simply haven't gotten to unpacking them all, and we don't know which one."

"I see." The man's face, as well as his response, showed that he didn't believe the girl's explanation about the map. Though Marge couldn't understand the reason for the story that Sally told, she said nothing. Then Natacha entered the room again, to clear away the remnants of the meal. Grant Whitcomb called her to his side, and spoke softly and rapidly in a language neither of the girls could understand. It must have been some sort of Indian dialect, made up of throaty guttural sounds. Natacha seemed to comprehend him though, and nodded in response to several questions.

Watching the bald-headed man and the aged woman. Marge fancied Natacha showed signs of embarrassment if such a thing were possible. She hung her head, as if in shame, then tried to offer explanation in the same tongue Whitcomb used. The man acted quite angry at times during the strange speech, and when he finished with a pointing gesture, Natacha slumped from the room without a reply.

"I told her," Whitcomb interpreted, "that she'd put you girls in the wrong room. I intended to put you both in the room on the other side of the hall. It's much bigger and you'll find the bed lots better."

"But we're satisfied with our room," objected Sally.

"No trouble at all to change. She'll move your things for you. I want you to have the best we can offer while you're here." Grant Whitcomb's air fell short of being magnanimous because it didn't seem to ring true. In fact, nothing seemed to ring quite true about the man. When he was angry, Marge had the impression he was putting on an act. When he spoke genially, she felt he used the tone to mask some other inner feeling. She couldn't understand him at all, but decided that until morning, she wouldn't try to understand him. She was badly in need of sleep and the sooner she got to bed, the better she'd be satisfied. She suggested that it might be bedtime.

"Natacha will have you moved in just a couple of minutes. You might like separate rooms, if that's the case, I'll—"

"Oh, no," blurted Sally, "we want to be together."

"That's what I thought."

Would Natacha move their things without finding

the map beneath the rug? If so, would the girls have the chance to get into that first room and retrieve the map? Was it possible that Whitcomb suspected that the map had been hidden in the room and wanting it himself, used this means of having the room un-occupied so he could search it? Marge was in confu-sion at the many, many things that crowded her mind. That map had caused no end of trouble. She almost wished it wasn't in existence, yet the future of the sisters depended so much on finding the gold claim it represented. Each time the map was mentioned, there seemed further proof of its tremendous value.

Down the hallway, Natacha was crossing from one room to a room on the opposite side of the hall, heavily loaded with the luggage of the girls. In a moment she returned to the first room to reappear, crossing the hall with all the unpacked clothing. She disappeared beyond the door of the new quarters of the girls, and then there came a shout of genuine surprise and terror.

It was like the scream of a tortured soul, freezing both girls to their chairs and bringing Whitcomb leaping to his feet, while his right hand scooped a heavy six-gun from a shelf behind him. He whirled, holding the gun ready, pointed down the hallway. "What's the matter?" Whitcomb bellowed like an angry bull.

"What's the matter with you, you old hag?"

Natacha came running, waving her arms in wild confusion, jabbering in her native tongue. The girls could make out just a single word in the middle of her gibberish. "Hoodoo."

"What do you mean?"

"Face! Face with mask!"

From the jumble of mixed English and Indian words that followed, the girls gathered that Natacha had seen a man's face, partly concealed by a mask, peering into the room through the window.

Then from somewhere outside the house, a ringing shout of "Heigh-Yo Silver," was followed by a thundering tatto of pounding hoofs receding. It was a familiar voice to the girls. Somehow it seemed to thrill them with an exultation—a feeling that there was at least *one* individual upon whom they could count. The masked rider wasn't as far from the ranch as they'd supposed. Strange, too, that they should feel that way. They had reason to believe the masked man a leader of a band of terrorists, and yet . . . both girls felt glad that he was near.

Whitcomb returned to the table, from the window to which he'd dashed, following the shout of the Lone Ranger. He needlessly assured the girls that they should not worry, he'd not let the masked man get at them. "But," he finished, "remember what I told you. *Don't leave this place alone!*" Marge wondered if that was a warning . . . . or a threat. She still wondered, when with Sally she took possession of the second bedroom Natacha showed them, and closed the door behind her.

CHAPTER XI

The Hooded Leader

"There was something about him I didn't like and didn't trust, that's why I fibbed about the map!" Sally was explaining her statements after the girls were in the room to which Natacha led them.

The room was slightly larger than the first, and furnished in much the same way. It was hardly different enough to call for switching bags and clothing as Grant Whitcomb ordered old Natacha to do. The rug on the floor, hooked and oval like the other, went back suddenly as Sally had an inspiration. "Nope," she muttered, after a close inspection of the floor, "there's no trap door in this room." She replaced the rug, speaking as she did so. "I wonder if he had us changed because of that trap door? Maybe he didn't want us to find it. I wonder what he'd say if he knew we'd already found it?"

"I'm more worried about the map than I am the floor," replied Marge. "The map is in the first room, and there's no way we can go there after it, without answering a lot of questions."

For a moment Sally's forehead wrinkled in perplexity. Then she said, "I might be able to sneak into that room after Uncle Grant has gone to bed. N—no, that wouldn't do. If he caught me, he would ask questions. *I'm going after it right now!*" She picked up the comb she'd used a short time previously. "In case anyone says anything, I'll just say Natacha overlooked this."

Marge began to remonstrate, but knowing Sally well, felt that it would be hopeless. Besides, she wanted desperately to have that map with her. The same thing that aroused Sally's vague suspicions, impressed Marge. Grant Whitcomb hadn't acted in the least bit natural.

Sally opened the door, and peeked out. She saw no sign of either her uncle or Natacha. Then she boldly crossed the five-foot hall and entered the opposite room.

While waiting for her sister to return, Marge reviewed the conversation with Grant Whitcomb. After seeing his nieces for the first time, his questions concerning their life, the affairs of his only relative, his brother, and the events surrounding his brother's death had been most casual. Marge had the impression that he'd asked them merely to fill in conversation. His interest in the girls' replies had been nil.

Another thing Marge didn't like—her uncle's moodiness. She didn't like the sudden changes from a genial host to a cold-voiced man whose face was the hardest and sternest she had ever seen. A man whose anger might become a thing to fear.

Then Sally returned, and closed the door behind her with a grin. "Nothing to it. Here's the map." She held the bit of paper toward Marge who took it and tucked it in the toe of the shoe she'd just removed. "That's a good place for it," commended Sally. "What's more, it'll bear out what I told our uncle. It might easily have dropped into your shoe while it was packed in the grip."

"It will do until morning anyway," agreed Marge. "I think we'll have the chance to find out more about this place tomorrow."

Sally nodded. "What," she asked, "did you think about the masked man?"

Marge looked at her sister curiously.

"Did you believe what Uncle said?"

The older of the girls shook her head slowly. "I—I can't make myself believe that man is really bad, in spite of the mask."

"Good!" Sally was emphatic. "That's how I felt."

Then she yawned a great and satisfying yawn, and began removing her clothes. Both girls were too tired to talk for very long. The bed was comfortable and the cool night air coming through the open window an invitation to a good night's sleep. Back to back, the sisters burrowed deep beneath the coverings and the last thing Marge was conscious of, was her sister's sleepy mutter, "I'm disappointed in this room, we don't have any trap door in the floor."

The girls slept soundly, but if they had been able to overhear the things that were talked of outside the house that night, they would have understood why the place was called a "Hoodoo Ranch," . . . they would have fled from there as fast as possible, pre-

ferring death from hunger and exhaustion on the
prairie to what the future held!

When the Lone Ranger and Tonto left the girls
a couple of miles from their uncle's ranch, it was the
masked man's plan to return to the clearing in the
woods. For several miles, he rode in silence while the
darkness gathered. From time to time he glanced at
Tonto, but made no comment because the Indian
seemed to be deep in thought.

Though the Lone Ranger didn't know it, Tonto
was debating with himself. He was trying to arrive at
a decision as to whether or not it would be best to tell
the rumors he'd heard about the Whitcomb Ranch.
After all, it was Natacha who had brought the stories
to the Indians who had related it to Tonto. Natacha
might be too old to think clearly, her hearing might
be dulled with her age, and her eyesight might be dim.
Things told by old Natacha might not be worth re-
counting. If Tonto told them to his friend, he might
be laughed at, and Tonto could not stand scorn and
ridicule. Still, the Lone Ranger had yet to laugh at
Tonto. If, after all, there really *was* something
about the ranch that wasn't as it should be, the masked
man should know it.

There was a strong dividing line between the things
the Indians knew and those that came to the attention
of the white men in the region. The Indians told
things among themselves that never crossed the line
to become the white man's knowledge. Many times
it had been Tonto who had brought facts of this sort

over the border. But other times, the things that Tonto told were facts. This knowledge he had of the Whitcomb ranch was merely hearsay, and the stories were started by an old crone—Natacha. Tonto would have thought no more about it, if Sally hadn't mentioned what the cowmen in the stagecoach station told her.

Finally Tonto arrived at his decision. The Lone Ranger looked at him with curiosity when he broke the long silence of the ride with, "Me want talk."

"Go ahead, Tonto. What do you want to talk about? I suppose it's time we stopped long enough to see what food remains in our saddle bags."

"That not it."

"No?"

Tonto rode another hundred yards in silence while the masked man waited patiently for him to continue. Then he started, and once begun, he talked for many miles without a stop. He told every detail of the things Natacha had said about the Whitcomb ranch. He explained how most of the Indians knew the stories that were rife, and how no Indian would risk scorn by telling them to white men. Halfway through his recital, Tonto had to stop his horse to remain with that of the Lone Ranger. The masked man was genuinely interested, urging him to go on, pressing him for details. "And why," he interrupted once, "hasn't Natacha had someone investigate these things?"

Tonto answered by telling the masked man a thing

he should have known. Indians had long since learned to keep to their own affairs, and not interfere with *anything* done by white men. "I don't understand it," the Lone Ranger said, when Tonto finished. "That sounds as if Whitcomb might be involved in some pretty shady dealings!"

Tonto nodded in agreement.

"And that doesn't check up at all. His reputation has always been the best a man could have. Honest as the day is long, a good man to work for, a square shooter, and a good cattle raiser."

"That why me not tell this before now."

"Grant Whitcomb has lived on that ranch for as long as I can remember. Some folks think he's a little strange, because of the way he keeps to himself, but that's his business." He swung his horse around, "We're going back to that ranch, Tonto."

Tonto was pleased with the decision. He took a quick glance at the trail ahead, then swung his own white horse about to head back the way they'd come; to return to the ranch that was labeled "Hoodoo."

"We'll not remain there for long, Tonto. I just want to make sure the girls are safe and sound in their uncle's care, then we'll start again for the woods. We can camp there tonight and tomorrow if the outlaws aren't around, have a look at the clearing near Flynn's Bluff and see what there is to see!"

Everything, when the Lone Ranger and Tonto arrived at the ranch as silently as possible, seemed as it should be.

Disliking the idea of being something of a prowler, but feeling that the end justified the means, the Lone Ranger crept close to the house and peered in at one window. The sight that met his eyes was reassuring. The two girls, seemingly in the best of spirits, were at the table in conversation with the uncle. The man was smilingly genial, and both girls seemed to have enjoyed the meal they'd finished.

Then, seeing another lighted window, the masked man and Tonto crept along the side of the low house until the square of light was just above their heads. Looking into what was a bedroom, they saw old Natacha entering with the property of the girls. She handled the things carefully, putting each article in its proper place. Her lips were moving, as she mumbled to herself!

"The girls are safe, and everything is being done to make them comfortable," the Lone Ranger whispered to his Indian companion.

"Old woman, talkum to herself," growled the other in disapproval as if that settled the matter of Natacha's reliability.

The two were about to leave, when Natacha saw the masked face at the window. It was then that she had screamed in fear, bringing Whitcomb to his feet in a hurry. Satisfied that all was well, at least for the time being, and anxious to get to the outlaws' camp, the Lone Ranger mounted his horse and rode away with Tonto following.

It was not until two hours later, when Marge and

Sally were sound asleep, that a short, squat man with huge chest and shoulders left the Whitcomb house. His head and neck were covered by a black hood. He wore a sombrero over the hood, and moved silently toward the corral. As he saddled and mounted a horse, he chuckled softly to himself, "I'll have a few things to tell the boys tonight." Then after a pause he added, "And maybe a trap to set for this Lone Ranger, if only he plans to go to the clearin'!"

The leader of the Night Legion was on his way to meet his men!

CHAPTER XII

Council of War

A scorching sun beat down from a copper-colored sky. Heat waves rose from the hot, dusty road that divided the two rows of unpainted, sun-bleached buildings that made up the town of Showdown. Few people stirred there during the heat of the day, and those who did, moved slowly and stopped frequently to slake their thirst and wash the dust from their throats. The cafes did a steady business, and there was generally a group of men to be found gathered on the porch of the general store, swapping lies or relating new horrors of the Night Legion.

It was here that riders from the Whitcomb ranch had waited in vain on the previous afternoon for the arrival of Marge and Sally. It was in Showdown that the arrival of the unguided horses and the empty stage brought news of tragedy along the trail.

Dust billowed from the heels of Sheriff Cook as he dismounted from his horse and tossed the reins about the hitch-rack. "Anyone in my office?" he inquired of loungers on the porch. A couple of men nodded, as if speaking called for too much effort on a hot day. Another responded verbally, "Walrus an' that new Dep'ty yuh hired from Texas is in thar."

Sheriff Cook nodded in approval. His heels clumped on the porch. "Holdin' a council of war this mornin'," he informed his friends. "It was bad enough when these Night Legion killers stole cattle, but it was a dang sight worse when they took tuh cold-blooded murder. But NOW," he said emphatically, "that they've kilt two of my deputies, by damn, they're goin' tuh PAY!"

The door slammed behind him and he went inside leaving those on the porch to pass the word that Sheriff Cook was madder than he'd ever been before. Without a glance in either direction, Sheriff Cook strode to his desk, sat in his chair and leaned back. He pushed his black hat far back on his head, revealing a shock of stiff, iron-gray hair. Every part of his face, the thin, stern mouth, the heavy jaw, the bristling mustache and the long, straight nose, denoted honesty and fearlessness. His eyes were deep and brown, overshadowed by thick eyebrows, slightly gray to match his hair. His voice, when he greeted the two men who had been there ahead of him, was soft, his words carefully chosen, but he gave the impression of one who was not only used to giving commands, but also used to seeing those commands carried out to the letter.

He unbuttoned his vest, then slid the ivory-handled .45 from his holster and placed it on the desk. Sheriff Cook had a habit of making himself as comfortable as possible when there was an important matter to discuss. It was frequently said of him, "when the

Sheriff takes his coat off and rolls up his sleeves, things happen."

It was not until the Sheriff finished with his personal affairs, and mopped his face with a huge handkerchief, that he paid the least attention to the two others in the office with him. From long association, old Walrus Lonergan knew what to expect, and sat with his chair tilted and nicely balanced against the wall, waiting patiently for his superior to get down to business.

Walrus fingered the long mustache for which he was named, while he looked at the uneasiness of the youthful, newly sworn in deputy. Tex Wilson was already tired of the inaction of waiting. Just before the arrival of Sheriff Cook, Tex had paced the floor with frequent pauses to light a cigarette, and a tailor-made one at that, only to take a few puffs then toss it in the brass cuspidor in the corner near the Sheriff's desk. Now Tex crossed and uncrossed his legs, raked a match on the bottom of his chair to light another cigarette, and seemed like a race horse at the barrier, anxious to get into action to hunt down the murderers of the four men on the stage trail.

During the time Sheriff Cook scanned through some letters on his desk, Walrus gave Tex Wilson a careful scrutiny. The fellow from the Lone Star State looked capable. In his stocking feet he'd have stood at least six-feet tall. His high-heeled boots added two inches to this. He was lean-faced and narrow-hipped, but his shoulders had a good breadth.

Walrus saw the metal star on Tex's vest, and though the old timer hated to share the honors of being a deputy with anyone, he was forced to admit grudgingly that Tex Wilson looked like he'd do! He wondered how fast Tex was with the six-gun. As the Sheriff finished with the mail the stage had brought in, Walrus paused in his mechanical chewing and spat toward the cuspidor. His aim was perfect. He scored a direct hit, and grinned toward Tex. "At least an eight-foot shot," he explained.

"All right, gents!" Sheriff Cook's voice brought both deputies to attention. "Now we can get down to facts." He pushed the papers from the top of his desk into a drawer and closed it. "Do you," he asked, looking at Tex Wilson, "understand just why yer bein' took on as a deputy?"

The Texan nodded slowly. "I shore do," he drawled. "Ah'm tuh take orders from you an' follow them orders to the letter."

"That's right, that's what yer tuh do, but do yuh know why I needed another deputy in a hurry last night?"

"Lost a couple men durin' the stage hold-up, didn't yuh, Sheriff Cook?"

"Right again."

"Ah happened tuh be on hand when the remains was brought in. Ah not only saw the dep'ties an' the guard an' driver, which same was drilled in cold blood without a chance tuh fight back, but ah also saw the outlaws that had gone down in the gun fight. I might go on record as sayin', Sheriff, that ah never seen a more ugly pair of polecats in mah entire life, an' they ain't a thing ah'd like more'n tuh line my gunsights on the rest of that outfit."

"They belonged to the Night Legion."

"Ah heard that."

"And the Night Legion drifted up this way from down where you came from. Maybe you didn't know that?"

Tex Wilson nodded. "Ah knowed that also, Sheriff Cook. Fact is, ah came up here fer the same reason. Them skunks killed my Paw!"

Walrus looked surprised at this. "Yuh didn't tell me *that* about yerself," he complained.

"Yuh didn't ask, Pardner, but the true fact is, ah'd have drilled them snakes on sight, even if it made me an outlaw tuh do it. Buzzards that'll torture a man with boot an' fist while he's hog-tied, then drill him between the eyes ain't deservin' of a legal trial an' hangin'."

Sheriff Cook broke in. "The law's on your side now, Tex Wilson, only be sure you're getting outlaws when you shoot."

Tex Wilson nodded. "Ah don't know much about what them Night Legion critturs done up around this country, but ah do know about 'em down where ah come from."

"If yuh ain't heard," blurted Walrus, "what they done around here, then by durn yuh ain't heard nothin'!" He spat another brown stream and scored another bull's-eye. Fancying he saw a glint of approval in Tex Wilson's eyes, he skidded his chair a couple feet further away, to prepare for his next shot. "Lemme tell him about 'em," he asked Sheriff Cook.

The Sheriff nodded and Walrus, eager to hold the attention of the man from Texas, began speaking. "It started a couple months ago when the Night Legion attacked Chuck Stillwater's place. They rid down roarin' wild an' shootin' hard, shot Chuck an' his wife an' set fire tuh the house."

"Like ornery Apaches," commented Tex Wilson.

"Worse!" Walrus seemed to speak with a voice of experience. "They kilt half a dozen of the waddies there, an' rid off, takin' all the cattle with 'em. Couple o' the boys died slow, an' had the chance tuh tell about these critturs with the black hoods on their heads." Walrus dramatized his story with many gestures.

When he finished Tex Wilson nodded. "The same bunch all right enough," he said, "but by the way, Pardner, I didn't get yore name."

Walrus gauged the distance to the cuspidor. "Jest call me Walrus," he said, then let go another brown stream of tobacco juice and grinned in self-approval. "Or yuh might call me Dead Shot!"

"The Stillwater raid was just the beginning," Sheriff Cook explained, taking up where Walrus left off. "Every night after that someone would go down before the guns of the Night Legion. It got to the point where folks didn't dare leave the house after dark, an' they was afraid tuh stay IN the house! It's been getting worse all the time! The worst of it is those killers don't leave folks alive when they're finished. Even when the Stillwater ranch riders was left alive, they didn't linger for very long, and couldn't tell much."

"Then there ain't no clues as tuh who these men might be?"

"No clues at all! There's no way of tellin' who they are, or no way of tellin' where they'll strike. It don't seem to matter if it's horses or cattle, money or jewels, they just take anything they c'n get their hands on. Now take that stagecoach, for example! There wasn't nothin' on THAT worth the stealin'!"

"A couple gals," said Walrus.

"But the girls weren't on the stage when the Night Legion attacked it. There wasn't any reason for them to wipe out the guard and driver and my deputies."

"I understand the girls was nieces of a rancher north o' here."

"That's right. They were comin' to live with Grant Whitcomb, he owns the Whitcomb ranch."

"And he had some men in town here tuh meet the girls, didn't he?"

"Yep."

"What'd they say when the wimmin folks weren't aboard?"

"Nothin'," interrupted Walrus. "Them Whitcomb riders are a curious lot o' men. They don't have nothin' tuh say tuh no one. They don't even take a drink! Would yuh believe it," he went on as if to him the thought were beyond comprehension, "them riders hired by Grant Whitcomb, hangin' around town all day in the hot sun, never took a single drink?"

"Whitcomb won't hire a drinkin' man," Sheriff Cook explained to Tex. "He's a curious sort himself, but I guess he pays his men top prices. They stick with him, don't talk to strangers, and obey orders."

"I don't savvy men like that," said Walrus shaking his head slowly. "They jest ain't natural."

"I could have explained to the men that the girls were safe," the Sheriff said, "but they didn't mention anything to me and I'm darned if I'll talk when folks don't want to hear me!"

"Where did the girls go?"

"The deputies that died left a note for me. It seems they met a man they knowed they could trust an' went with him. He took the girls off the stage, with the deputies help, and cut north across the plains before the robbery took place."

Walrus was gradually working up to another shot. From the corner of his eye, he watched Tex Wilson, so the young deputy from Texas wouldn't miss his show of skill. The old fellow was past the age when he could display a prowess with firearms or skilled horsemanship, and he was anxious to excite admiration of the things he could do. He caught Tex glancing in his direction and tried to appear casual as he spat once more. This time, however, his aim was short. He looked quickly at the Sheriff, saw the glare in his boss's eyes, and dropped his eyes, crestfallen. "Better fergit that nickname of 'Dead Shot,' " he muttered.

"So," said Tex Wilson finally, "there's the three of us to round up the Night Legion."

"Four," corrected Sheriff Cook. Tex looked at him questioningly. "Dave Sands is the fourth. He's a deputy about your age, but he ain't come in yet." Cook glanced at his big watch. "He should be back by now," he observed. "He went ridin' past the cottonwoods to call on old Joe Frisby."

Walrus undertook to explain Joe Frisby. "He's a sort of hermit crittur that lives alone in a shack. Every so often one of us rides over tuh his place tuh see if he's still alive, or if old age has got him an' he's needin' of a burial."

A cloud of dust rose past the window outside the office, and the shouts of the men on the porch told of a new arrival. A hearty, vibrant voice shouted a general greeting to the men and then the door burst open and Dave Sands, stamping dust from his boots, walked in, with his face set in a mask-like expression. He slammed the door, and walked straight to Sheriff Cook's desk. Dave Sands' face was streaked with sweat and dust. Foam flecks from a hard-ridden horse quivered on his clothing. In his gloved hand, he held a note which he slapped down on the desk of the Sheriff saying, "Read that, Sheriff, an' let me tell yuh it's the truth. I checked on it. Joe Frisby has been murdered!"

Walrus choked on his cud at the news Dave Sands brought in. Sheriff Cook reached across his desk, and took the note. There was dead silence while he read it slowly, digesting every crudely formed word. He could move quickly and with the agility of a panther when the need arose, but he also knew the value of making haste slowly, and making sure of each fact as he went along. Before he commented on the death of Joe Frisby, he wanted to study that note.

Walrus was sputtering volubly about the murder of the old man. "Never harmed a soul in his life, he wouldn't hurt a flee, he wouldn't do no one any harm an' there ain't nothin' he had that anyone would want. Who done it? Name the dirty, sawed off son of a polecat an' lemme at him with my six-guns blazin'!"

Tex stood up and eased close to Walrus. "Shut up," he whispered. Walrus stared wide-eyed at the speaker and stopped talking, but his mouth hung open at the sharpness that had come into the drawling voice of Tex Wilson. "When they's things tuh be done, keep still an' wait fer orders, don't sit there spoutin' like a doggone hen that's laid an egg!"

Sheriff Cook put down the note and looked at Sands. "Where'd you get it?"

"Fastened to a tree. It told about Joe Frisby, so I cut loose an' went there fast. I found him dead, just like the note says, then I come back here figurin' if we act fast we might get the killers!"

Sheriff Cook nodded his approval, then introduced Dave Sands to Tex Wilson. As the deputies clasped hands, each one saw things he admired in the other. Dave was slightly shorter than Tex. but broader through the chest. Each man had the same frank, sincere expression, and the clear eyes that denote perfect physical fitness. Instinctively, both Dave Sands and Tex Wilson knew they'd become close friends before very long.

"This note," explained Sheriff Cook, "tells that Joe Frisby has been murdered. It goes on tuh say that if I want to get the killer, I'll find him some time during the day, in a clearing just south of Flynn's Bluff. He'll likely be camped near there!"

"Then what're we waitin' for," burst out Walrus impetuously. "I know that clearin', I can take yuh right there. I've been there dozens of times. Let's git goin' so's I can git the chance tuh unlimber my gun." He spat without caring where he hit, then drew an old-fashioned pistol and waved it in the air.

Sheriff Cook glared at Walrus again. Slowly the noisy deputy holstered his gun, closed his mouth and resumed his seat. Then Cook looked at Dave Sands. "Bullet?" he queried.

Dave Sands nodded. "It was a bullet that got him, but he'd been knifed in the back as well. The knife wound was patched up first rate. The place was messed up somethin' fierce, though."

"How's that?"

"Busted furniture, bricks tore from the fireplace, boards ripped from the floor, an' the bed split open. Looked to me like whoever done the job was huntin' fer somethin'!"

"Money?"

"I thought so at first. Lots of folks has crazy notion; that every man that lives alone has a sight of money hid away somewhere, but after I studied things a while, I figgered it must've been somethin' a lot smaller than cash, on account of the places they'd been huntin'."

"For example?"

"Wal, yuh couldn't hide much cash in the leg of a chair or table, but they'd looked all them places. I thought it might have been somethin' like an important paper."

Sheriff Cook finally jammed his gun in leather, and buttoned his vest. "Boys, as long as we don't know who the members of the Night Legion are, we can't take in any more deputies because we don't know who tuh trust. That means there's jest the four of us!"

The others nodded their understanding. Though the death of Joe Frisby might be one more killing by the Night Legion, and though the Night Legion might number many score of members, the four must stand alone against them.

"You boys all set?"

Dave and Tex Wilson nodded. Walrus said, "You bet!" Then the quartette left the office to go to the clearing in the woods. The same clearing that the Lone Ranger planned to go to.

CHAPTER XIII

Capture and Escape

After the scorching hot stretch of open, dusty country between Showdown and the dense woods, the coolness of the trees came as a comforting and welcome relief to Sheriff Cook and his three aides. They rode in single file, breaking a trail through the timber with old Walrus taking the lead and guiding them toward the clearing near Flynn's Bluff. He seemed to know where he was going . . . to know the woods far better than any of the others. During the ride across the plains he'd told how in his younger days he had spent many days exploring the woods. He described the clearing in minute detail and explained how Flynn's Bluff came to get its name. He even knew of a cave in the Bluff right at the edge of the woods.

The quartette of lawmen were not the only ones who headed for the clearing. The Lone Ranger, coming from another direction, had the same place as a destination. He was doing precisely what the leader of the hooded men, the Boss of the Night Legion thought he'd do. He was going directly into the carefully planned trap, unaware of the note Dave Sands had found.

The Lone Ranger and Tonto were refreshed by a

good night's rest. It had been well past daybreak before they wakened, and the masked man recalled with amusement the disgust of Tonto when the Indian opened his eyes to find the sun already slanting through the leafy ceiling of their woodland camp. They might have slept even longer had it not been for Silver, but the great white stallion, unable to comprehend the breaking of day and the rising of the sun with his master asleep, had wakened the Lone Ranger by a gentle muzzling at the sleeping masked man's side.

The two made breakfast a hasty meal. Then, with their few utensils washed and stowed away in saddle bags, they were in the saddle and on their way toward the outlaws' camp of two nights previous. "It's just as well," the Lone Ranger said, "that we went back to the Whitcomb ranch last night. If we'd gone there in the darkness, it would have been pretty hard to find anything."

Tonto nodded grimly, still somewhat angry with himself for what he considered laziness in oversleeping darkness. "Plenty lawmen huntum clue," he muttered. "No one find-um!"

"That's just why I'm glad we're going there in daylight. It will be hard to read the signs about the camp in daylight, and it would be much harder at night."

For a time, the Indian rode in silence, the only sound being the hoofs of the horses on the soft loam of the woods. "Other lawmen," he said at length, "not live."

The Lone Ranger was well aware of this. Of all those who set out to run down the Night Legion, especially the leader, these two alone, the masked man and the Indian survived. The others were dead. He recalled the Texas Rangers who had died at the hands of the outlaws he sought, and his resolve to somehow stick to the trail until he ran the fiendish killers to earth was renewed!

The Boss didn't like loose ends. Well, he'd left one, when he failed in his attempts to get the Lone Ranger. That one loose end might be his undoing. Random thoughts passed through the masked man's mind while he followed Tonto through the forest. The Boss, he knew, was well aware of the loose end that dangled, and constant vigilance was needed to avoid the traps the Boss might set for him. Subconsciously, his senses were constantly attuned to pick up the least unusual sound or sight. The odor of a campfire would have brought him to a sudden halt, his guns would flash to readiness, and he would be alert and ready for action. The sound of a horse other than his own or Tonto's, the sight of any moving object in the forest would be caught by his alert attention.

The Lone Ranger didn't underestimate his adversary's power. He was fully aware of the fact that in the Boss of the Night Legion, he was pitted against the coldest, shrewdest, most calculating, and by far the most ruthless enemy of law and order the West had ever known. A man who was a leader of other men. A dominating king of the lawless band and one who was totally unknown, even to his most trusted lieutenants.

Yet, in Tonto, the Lone Ranger had an ally whose skill in reading trail signs, in interpreting the most insignificant mark on the ground and in following a spoor, was unsurpassed. Tonto would prove a tower of strength in any fight, and Tonto, he knew, would gladly lay down his life at any time for the cause of justice or for the Lone Ranger. He was counting on Tonto more than the Indian realized in making this return trip to the clearing. During the hand to hand battle of two nights before, he saw something Tonto had been too occupied to notice. He saw the only man among the outlaws who was hooded, making his escape. He knew, after discussing events with Tonto later, that this man was the Boss. He recalled the exact place where the Boss had left the camp and his men to fight their own fight, while he mounted his horse to escape among the trees. There must be footprints there. One single footprint would be enough for Tonto. Having seen it, studied it and measured it, the Indian would never forget it. One print might be all that was needed to identify the leader of the Night Legion.

They passed a trail which crossed at right angles to the course they were following.

"Joe Frisby's place is over that way, Tonto," commented the Lone Ranger.

"That right."

"As soon as we have a chance, we must send men there to give the poor old man a decent burial. Then we must tell the Sheriff of the county about the man we found hanging . . . tell him about that grave in the valley."

Tonto nodded agreement.

Then the two continued in silence for the better part of half an hour and finally they arrived at the clearing in the woods. In daylight it seemed smaller than it had during the night. It was a natural room, one of Nature's whims. A large slab of stratified rock had been deposited here in some dim distant age of the past. The centuries that followed had covered the rock with a layer of several inches of mud and clay; enough to support a grassy overgrowth, but not deep enough to afford trees a roothold.

The clearing was surrounded on all sides by giant trees whose branches, interwoven overhead, made a ceiling thirty feet above the ground. Traces of the camp were clearly visible—the charred remains of the fire, the indentations of horses' hoofs and here and there a deeper mark, where the hoofs of Silver had lashed down and struck the ground with terrific force.

The Lone Ranger and Tonto dismounted in the center of the clearing, and the masked man went directly to the place where he had last seen the Boss. Sure enough, the print was there. Several footprints of a heavy man with short but exceptionally broad feet. Best of all, the boot had a peculiar hobnail pattern that would make it easily recognized if seen again!

So intent were the two men in their inspection of the footprint, that for once their vigilance relaxed. A soft whinny from Silver should have warned them.

At almost any other time the uneasy sound of the big white horse would have found the masked man and the Indian whirling to one side, snatching at guns, ready to ward off unexpected attack, but now, before the actual footprint of the man they'd hunted for so long, the warning of the horse fell on deaf ears.

When the Lone Ranger first became aware of danger, it was too late to act. The sharp voice of Sheriff Cook cracked like a whip in the clearing. "H'ist yer hands, you're covered from all sides."

At first the Lone Ranger thought the order came from members of the Night Legion who had returned to their camp. He felt that any fast move would bring certain death roaring from half a dozen six-guns, so he lifted his hands slowly to shoulder level, then rose to his feet and turned toward the voice.

"Got yuh by thunder, we got yuh flatfooted." It was Walrus who spoke, gloating over the ease of the capture, and delighted to find but two men there where he thought he'd be against big odds.

The masked man studied the situation. He counted four men in all, each one holding a gun level. They were spread far apart so it was impossible to watch them all at one time. The badge on Sheriff Cook's vest caught his eye and despite the fact that he was captured by the law, he was glad to note that it wasn't the hooded men who'd come here. The law might unmask him, might put an end to all he hoped to do in the future, but he at least would have the chance to discuss matters before cold-blooded shooting cut him down. He could, even if jailed on suspicion, pass on what he'd learned to the lawmen, and hope they might carry on where he and Tonto left off.

He was about to speak when the tallest of the quartette spoke in a soft drawling voice, characteristic of Texas. "Mister, they jest ain't no use tryin' tuh put up no argument, either with yer tongue or guns. We'd a darn sight sooner shoot yuh here an' now, than take yuh tuh stand trial, an' all we need is a sudden move on yore part tuh do that same."

Tex Wilson spoke the truth, and the Lone Ranger knew it. He wondered just how the Sheriff's men happened to come here, and thought it would be a simple matter to establish his innocence of anything they might plan to charge him with. The next moment, however, split his theories wide open. He asked what charges he was to be arrested on. Sheriff Cook responded.

"Robbery and murder. We're holdin' you fer the murder of a man named Joe Frisby."

This was news to the Lone Ranger. "Joe Frisby?" he repeated questioningly. "I've had no part in the murder of that man."

"D'you deny you went near his place?" As he spoke, the Sheriff eyed the newly made footprints on the ground. "Take a look," he said to one of the deputies, "an' tell me if those match the prints at Frisby's shack."

Dave Sands studied them a moment, then said, "I'd stake my life on it."

There was no use denying the fact he'd been to Frisby's, so the Lone Ranger admitted it, then tried to explain just what took place when he got there. "It," he concluded, "was the Night Legion who killed Joe Frisby. We followed the hooded men to this clearing, then we had to leave in a hurry. We came back here today to examine the footprints of the Boss of the Night Legion." He indicated the peculiar footprint on the ground near where he stood. "I don't know how you happened to come here, but it is a fact, that you're going to let the real criminals escape if you waste time with me."

Sheriff Cook showed by his expression that he didn't believe a word of the masked man's story. For a moment, the Lone Ranger thought of explaining how he had gone to the lawman's office in Showdown, persuaded two of the deputies that he was actually working on the same side of the law as they were, and secured their aid in rescuing Sally and Marge. Then it struck him forcefully, that the deputies were dead. There would be no way to prove a story that would sound too fantastic for the Sheriff to believe.

"Take his guns," ordered Sheriff Cook. Tex Wilson stepped forward to disarm the masked man. Capture meant unmasking, it meant the end of everything he hoped to do. It might mean even worse than jail. As the facts stood there was a strong case against him, and the folks in Showdown, aroused to a fever pitch of red hate for the outlawry in the region, would be unlikely to wait for trial in the court of law. A lynching would be practically inevitable.

It wasn't that the Lone Ranger feared death. He knew that some day he would go down, fighting for the things for which he stood, but there was so much yet to be done. So much that needed doing that he felt himself qualified to accomplish. The approach of Tex Wilson seemed like the approach of doom to him. No, he would not let himself be captured. A quick glance showed him his horse standing close at hand, and a couple of yards beyond it, Tonto's horse. Tonto, he knew, would fall into perfect alignment with whatever he attempted. Tex Wilson was but six feet from him, when he barked a sharp command.

His voice carried a ring that Silver knew! The great stallion, carefully and painstakingly trained for just such an emergency, went into action. His great muscles leaped into play, like a steel spring suddenly released from tension. Silver left the ground with all four feet at once, in a lunging spring against Tex Wilson. The other three men, watching the masked man, didn't see the horses move for the split second before Tex crashed to the ground. The deputy's sudden yell of surprise attracted the attention of the others, and it was in that instant that the Lone Ranger and Tonto acted. They leaped forward, knocking down the guns of Sheriff Cook and Dave Sands, while Silver, in his charge rushed Walrus to one side, and to break his fall, the old-timer dropped his gun.

These men, however, were lawmen. Temporarily opposed to the Lone Ranger through their misunder-

standing of the situation, they were none the less fighting for the same things he fought for, and he didn't
want to hurt them. He shouted to Silver, who was
already rearing to strike down with those sharp fore-
hoofs at Tex Wilson, prone on the ground. Silver responded, swinging quickly to one side, to drop his
hoofs harmlessly a scant foot from the lawman.

Then, for a long two minutes, there was a mad melee
of flying hands, arms and legs. The old deputy named
Walrus reaching to retrieve his gun, saw it spin ten
yards away when a fast shot from the Lone Ranger's
gun struck it squarely. Tonto's fist smashed down on
Dave Sands' forearm, paralyzing it with pain, making him unable to use a weapon for an hour to come.
The masked man's weapon spoke again, and the gun
dropped by Sheriff Cook was smashed beyond repair.
"To the saddle," cried the Lone Ranger, suiting the
action to the word by leaping to the back of Silver.
Tonto, in the saddle, shouted a command, and his
horse was under way. The Lone Ranger shouted
"Heigh-Yo Silver." Sheriff Cook, burning with fury
at the surprise attack, grabbed Dave Sands' gun from
the grass where it had fallen. He swung to fire pointblank at the flash of white horseflesh that thundered
past him, heading for the woodland depths, when the
Lone Ranger's shout came to him. "Silver!" That
"Heigh-Yo Silver" rang a familiar chord. The Sheriff
held his fire.

Walrus was on his feet, fumbling in his efforts to
make use of the gun dropped by Tex Wilson, but Tex

beat him to it, grabbed the weapon and jerked it to bear on the fast moving horse that was just visible through the dense growth.

"Hold it," barked the Sheriff. "Don't fire."

"Shoot, shoot him," screamed old Walrus. "What're yuh waitin' for? Let him have it. Bring him down! He's one of the Night Legion."

"Night Legion nothing!" Sheriff Cook's shout topped that of Walrus. "That man ain't in the Night Legion. He said, 'Heigh-Yo Silver!' *That was the Lone Ranger!*"

His modesty made the Lone Ranger totally unaware of the way his ringing cry had spread throughout the region. He had no way of knowing Sheriff Cook's new attitude toward him. As far as the Lone Ranger knew, his sudden burst for freedom had made both him and Tonto outlaws, sought by the men of Showdown for the murder of Joe Frisby. Now, he must be more careful than ever as he tracked down the Boss of the Night Legion. Capture now meant certain death by the hangman's rope, and the only way to clear himself, was to bring the *real* murderers of old Joe to justice.

CHAPTER XIV

A Call on the Sheriff

Breaking through the woods in flight from the law-men, the Lone Ranger and Tonto took every precaution to hide their trail. They doubled back on their tracks, set out false leads, and avoided places where the ground would retain the prints of their horses' hoofs. Whenever they came to a small spring-fed stream of water, they rode through it, following its course for quite a distance, so that even bloodhounds would have a hard time in pursuing them very far.

They traveled for several hours, heading in the general direction of the Whitcomb ranch despite the many times they broke their course. The masked man had long since given up his original plan of following the tracks made by the Boss's horse. Sheriff Cook and his men made such a course impossible. The lawmen, however, had given the Lone Ranger food for thought. He reasoned they had not just *happened* to come upon that clearing. They must have been sent there by someone who figured the Lone Ranger and Tonto would return. None but members of the Night Legion knew that the masked man had been in Frisby's shack. None others knew he'd found that clearing. It was logical, then, to suppose that members of the Night

Legion sent the Sheriff there to trap him, if and when he should return to the clearing.

The Lone Ranger wondered why Sheriff Cook and his men had waited until today to go to the clearing in the woods! He knew, from observation of the ground and the prints it still retained, that the lawmen hadn't been there previously. Yet, unless the one who sent them there was well aware of the masked man's movements on the previous day, they would have assumed that he'd go there the day following the battle with the hooded men. He hadn't. He'd been occupied with the delivery of the sisters to their uncle's ranch. Someone knew this, and the only ones who could have known it, were the men at the ranch. All things considered, the Night Legion seemed to be in some way associated with the Whitcomb ranch: the Hoodoo ranch.

"We'll get there as soon as we safely can," the Lone Ranger told the Indian. "I don't know exactly what we'll do when we arrive, but I want to have a look around and see if we can find any footprints that match those made by the Boss."

Tonto nodded silently. He, too, had for the past two hours been deep in thought. He asked the question the Lone Ranger had been considering for some time. "How Sheriff know we go-um to place in woods?"

The masked man explained his deductions. "They didn't just happen there, Tonto, they were sent there."

"Mebbe Sheriff in Night Legion!" Tonto commented.

This, too, had been a passing thought of the Lone Ranger but he'd discarded it long since. The Sheriff and his men were a far, far different type than the murderous fiends he'd fought with hand to hand in the clearing. He shook his head. "No, Tonto, I don't think that, but I do think, in fact, I'm almost sure of it, we'll find the Boss either close to the Whitcomb ranch, or in the town of Showdown."

"Who know-um we go to clearing?"

"I've been trying to think."

"You tell-um girls we go-um there."

"The girls, that's right. They knew where we were planning to go. They thought we started for there when we left them last evening, then they must have heard about us being near their house last night. If they reasoned it out at all, they'd realize that it would have been too late for us to go there last night, so we'd be likely to go there today."

"That right."

"The girls, of course, can't possibly be involved in the Night Legion. They've just come to this part of the country. But their uncle would hear everything they had to tell."

"Mebbe make-um guess who Boss is."

The Lone Ranger glanced at his companion. He knew just what Tonto thought and what the Indian implied. "No," he responded. "Grant Whitcomb can *not* be a member of the Night Legion."

Tonto looked across the narrow space that separated the two white horses. "Why?" he asked.

"Grant Whitcomb has been on his ranch for years. We can find dozens of people who will swear he hasn't left it for any length of time. The Boss of the Night Legion hasn't been in this country more than a few weeks. Remember, Tonto, he started his work in Texas. We followed him from there."

Tonto looked perplexed. But for this one point, many things seemed to indicate Grant Whitcomb. Stories of the weird things at the ranch, the way Whitcomb's men remained aloof and apart from all the other cowboys. The close seclusion of the Whitcomb ranch, and yet, what the Lone Ranger said was true. Grant Whitcomb couldn't have been in Texas when the outrages of the Night Legion were prevalent there, and at his ranch at the same time. Grant Whitcomb could not be the Boss they sought.

Tonto suddenly recalled something. "Wait," he muttered. His right hand slid beneath the buckskin jacket he wore and in a moment, after fumbling at some secret pocket, he withdrew his hand, guided his horse closer to the masked man's and said, "Here, you take-um."

The Lone Ranger reached out, and Tonto dropped a button in his open hand. He examined it closely. It was a fancy glass button, such as some men wore on their vests. Still clinging to it were a few strands of thread, and the pattern of the button was unique.

"Where did you get this?" he asked the Indian.

"Find-um in clearing, close to footprint of Night Legion Boss."

The Lone Ranger recalled seeing Tonto reach for something on the ground, but it was at that moment that the Sheriff's voice had ordered them to lift their hands and until now he'd forgotten to ask what Tonto had seen.

"This button," the Lone Ranger said slowly, "might be an even more important clue than the footprint. Of course, we aren't certain it came from the vest of the Boss, but if you found it near where he stood . ."

Tonto nodded.

"If we can only find the vest this came from," thought the Lone Ranger.

The woods were thinner now, as the two men reached the edge that bordered on a stretch of open country which extended due east to the Whitcomb rangeland, and southeast to the town of Showdown. Once in that open country, it would be practically impossible to keep their trail concealed.

"Whoa," commanded the Lone Ranger. Silver halted and Tonto's horse, accustomed to following the masked man's, did likewise.

The afternoon was well advanced. Grant Whitcomb's house and the town of Showdown were about the same distance from the Lone Ranger and Tonto, and it would be dark before either place could be reached. For a moment the Lone Ranger was undecided. "If," he muttered, "we head for the ranch, we'll not be able to do much hunting for footprints in the dark. If we go to Showdown, the darkness won't interfere with what I want to do. In fact, it will be a help."

"What you go-um to town for?" asked Tonto.

"Sheriff Cook will be there."

The Indian looked perplexed. The entire day since leaving the clearing, had been spent in avoiding Sheriff Cook and his men. Why then did the Lone Ranger suggest going to the stern-faced lawman?

"From here," observed the Lone Ranger, gazing through the slits in his mask at the level, open country extending as far as he could see, "we can head for Showdown. We planned to go to Whitcomb's place, because we thought Sheriff Cook went to the clearing because he was sent there by someone who wanted to trap us."

Tonto agreed, "That right."

"But," continued the masked man, "if Sheriff Cook was not sent there by someone, then our entire idea is worthless. Everything we suspect about the ranch would be wrong. There wouldn't be any reason to suspect that the Boss is in close touch with affairs at the ranch."

This, Tonto knew, was true. It had never been the Lone Ranger's style to go ahead on pure guesswork. Perhaps one of the reasons for his success in tracking down other criminals and in serving justice as he'd done before, was the fact that he made sure of each point as he went along, taking nothing on assumption and basing none of his conclusions on guesswork. Now, before he went to the Grant Whitcomb ranch, he wanted to go southeast to Showdown and interview the Sheriff.

"I want to get him alone," he said, referring to Sheriff Cook. "There are a couple of questions he alone can answer." He swung his horse southeast, prodded gently with his heel and the white stallion lunged ahead, carrying the Lone Ranger toward the town of Showdown with Tonto following a half-length behind.

During their ride back to town after a futile two hour search of the woods, the Sheriff's deputies were in a vile humor. Tex Wilson and Dave Sands had little to say, but their clouded faces showed how they felt at being outwitted by the flashing action of the Lone Ranger and his horse. Walrus did most of the talking, and his expressions were colorful to say the least. He promised dire things the next time he met up with the masked man and was profuse in explanations, punctuated by picturesque cuss-words, for his failure to get at least one shot at the fugitives.

Sheriff Cook's face was set in an expressionless mask. Occasionally it softened as a look of amusement twinkled in his eyes, but this was nothing more than a fleeting change to be immediately replaced by the grim sternness that indicated how he felt regarding the outrages of the Night Legion and the disappointment he felt at not having at least a few of the hooded men roped with him on his return to Showdown. "Shut your mouth," he finally warned Walrus.

"But the way them two got clear, they wouldn't never o' done it, if I'd been myself. I was chokin' on some swallered t'baccy juice jest at the same second them hosses jumped. Otherwise they wouldn't o' catched me sleepin'!"

"I didn't want them two, anyhow," growled Cook. "That masked man was the Lone Ranger, an' there ain't no call tuh take *him* tuh the calaboose! Thing that makes me sore is tuh think of spendin' the hull day ridin' tuh that clearin' an' back again an' not seein' hide nor hair of them hooded killers."

"If you didn't want them two," retorted Walrus with the freedom of long friendship with his superior, "why in tunket did yuh have us beatin' down the woods huntin' fer him?"

"Because I want tuh speak to him! If they's any man alive that's capable of turnin' up the Boss of the Night Legion, that Lone Ranger is the man!" He swung in the saddle to eye the two deputies who rode behind him. "I'd swap all three of you, an' three more like yuh, tuh have the Lone Ranger ridin' with me."

This didn't help to lift the state of mind of Tex and Dave.

Little more was said during the ride back to Showdown. It was well past dark when the quartette arrived. Walrus headed for the handiest café to relate his adventure with many additional details, figments of his vivid imagination, to his friends. Tex and Dave went off together to discuss the day's ride and talk about things in general, comparing notes on their respective backgrounds, and furthering a friendship that had started only that morning. Sheriff Cook, an old campaigner who knew the value of rest when the opportunity was at hand, went to his home and turned in for the night.

Something seemed to tell the Sheriff that there would be strenuous times in the days ahead. With the Lone Ranger in the vicinity, hounding the members of the Night Legion, open warfare between the hooded men and the law-abiding people of the community might break out at any moment. He didn't know exactly what he did expect, but he had a vague feeling that he'd do well to rest and sleep now, while he had the chance.

He didn't know how long he slept. He wakened suddenly and sat bolt upright in his bunk. For a moment he was confused, but as his brain cleared and the fog of deep sleep rolled back, he wondered what had wakened him. Something, that was sure. He listened intently there in the darkness, but heard no sound except the chirp of crickets, the distant revelry in the cafés and the dismal howl of a wolf.

He judged by the sounds from the cafés that it must be close to midnight. Then a strange sound came to his highly tuned ears. It was faint, barely audible, yet he was certain the sound was made by someone creeping along the ground, close to his home. Careful to make no sound, Sheriff Cook reached for the gun belt that was looped over the chair beside his bed. He drew his weapon from the holster, thinking as he did so, of the other gun that had been smashed by the Lone Ranger's bullet.

He heard the sound outside again. It seemed nearer to the front, as if someone were creeping around from the rear, to gain the unbarred door. Holding his gun beneath the covers on his bed, to muffle the metallic click, Cook drew back the hammer, then brought the gun out again, and held it steady, pointed at the doorway of his one-room house. There was a slight clawing sound against the heavy wood of the door, as if someone outside were fumbling for the latch.

Moonlight streaming through the window fell in a square patch on the bed, bathing the Sheriff's head and shoulders in a faint reflected light. The door started inward, but the deep, stern voice of a man rang from the Sheriff's side.

"Don't fire the gun, you might hurt someone!"

That voice, Sheriff Cook knew it well! He swung to his left, to see the head and shoulders of a man outlined in the window.

At that instant, the door opened and Tonto came into the room. Sheriff Cook, when he realized the trick that had been played, grinned directly at the man in the window who covered him. "Pretty slick," he commented in approval. "You had the redskin make just enough noise to keep my attention on the door, while you got the drop on me through the window, but come on inside, Lone Ranger, in the name of goodness come in and consider yourself more than welcome!"

Tonto, not entirely trusting the Sheriff, despite the ring of sincerity in his voice, kept a gun leveled while the tall, masked man skirted the house and came in through the door. "How did you know who I was?" he demanded of the Sheriff.

"Recognized your voice as that of the man in the clearing today, and I knew who you were there when I heard what you said to your horse."

"Do you still suspect me of the murder of Joe Frisby?"

The Sheriff shook his head. "Nope."

"I came here," stated the Lone Ranger, "for information. I now have hopes of getting what I came for, without too much trouble. I think you understand that I'm working for the same cause you are?"

Again the Sheriff nodded. His gun hand was relaxed, still gripping his weapon, but allowing it to rest upon the blanket of his bed.

"How did you," demanded the masked man, "happen to go to the clearing today? Was it your own idea or did someone send you?"

"I was sent by a note a deputy brought in after finding Joe Frisby dead."

The Lone Ranger's suspicions about the Whitcomb ranch were well founded! "Was the note signed?" he asked.

"Nope."

"Have you any idea who wrote it?"

"No idea, except this. Now I'm darn sure it was written by one of the Night Legion that figured you to return to the clearing and wanted me on hand to shoot it out with you. Whichever one of us was killed, it'd be one less against the Night Legion."

The Lone Ranger was about to ask another question when a yell sounded from somewhere down the road outside. He thought it was the oldest of the deputies, and he was right.

Walrus, on his way home from the café with several friends, sighted the two white horses near the Sheriff's house. "Thar's the hosses of them two," he yelled at the top of his voice. He'd taken just enough strong liquor to confuse and muddle his thoughts, and he still clung to the impression that the horses were owned by men who were wanted by the law.

"I couldn't mistake them hosses," Walrus went on, "come on boys an' surround the Sheriff's house, thar's where them critturs are at."

Every word the old man uttered, came clearly to the three inside the home of Sheriff Cook! "You'd better get away," Cook snapped. "The rest of the boys around here don't understand your work as I do. They're coming on the run."

There could be no doubt of this. Other voices added to the clamor started by old Walrus, and they were coming closer every second.

"But I must know," shouted the masked man, "who wears a blue vest. . ."

"No time," barked the Sheriff. He snatched at the drawer of a small table and it came all the way out to drop with a crash on the floor. "I'll give you the note!"

He was on the floor, brushing aside odds and ends that spilled from the drawer. When he stood in his bare-feet he thrust a piece of paper toward the Lone Ranger. "Here's the note."

The men were close to the house now, shouting words of encouragement to the Sheriff, thinking per-haps, he was at that moment in danger of his life. But quite the reverse was the case. The Sheriff not only was in no personal danger, he was interested on-ly in the safety of the one man in all the world he felt was capable of combating the Boss of the Night Leg-ion. "Take the note, study it when you get the chance, but now, in Heaven's name, get away from here while you have the chance."

The Lone Ranger jammed his gun into the holster and took the paper. He knew there was no chance to inquire about the man who wore a blue vest which had one button missing. He muttered a word of thanks, and streaked for the door, Tonto close behind him.

As the two covered the yards that separated them from their horses, guns barked on their right. They leaped to the saddles, amid the shouting of men and sharp commands to stand still, while more guns spoke and bullets zoomed close. "Heigh-Yo Silver," came the masked man's shout, and the two white horses were gone!

Half a dozen men, headed by old Walrus fired blind-ly at the fugitives, but having no horses at hand, were unable to give chase. Instead, they burst into Sheriff Cook's house, all talking at once!

Cook's voice rose above the others in an order to quiet down. "What in the devil's the matter with you, boys, raisin' such a rumpus in the middle of the night?"

Walrus tried to speak, but in his excitement with his tongue thickened by fiery liquor, he jabbered incoherently. "Aw calm down," the Sheriff said at length. "There's no call to get so excited. Now you boys clear out of here and let me get some sleep."

"B-b-but what . . what . . . " stammered Walrus, "what . . what was you doin' here? Wha . . what was them two men . . . "

"All that I was doin'," broke in the Sheriff, "was addin' a couple of deputies to get the Night Legion. Now vamoose!"

The men asked a couple more questions, which the Sheriff evaded, and then drifted out of the house somewhat disappointed at the let-down. When they had gone, Cook once more settled down in bed, and grinning broadly in the dark thought, "I'd swap a hundred men, to have the Lone Ranger on my side."

CHAPTER XV

SOUNDS IN THE NIGHT

Their first night's sleep on Grant Whitcomb's ranch was a rather broken one for Marge and Sally. When they turned in following the late supper and the visit with their uncle, the sisters thought they'd drop to sleep at once, but they were too tired to do so. Their nerves were taut, and every muscle screamed complaint after the torturous ride across the plains. Just as Marge was dozing, Sally nudged her, rousing her to listen to sounds outside the house.

There were men's voices, too far away to understand, but unquestionably something was going on. Quite a number of horses were assembled, and for a quarter of an hour both girls sat close to the window trying to hear what went on. The men were on the opposite side of the house, so they couldn't be seen by the nieces of Grant Whitcomb. Then with creaking of leather and jangling of spurs the sounds faded out.

Ordinarily Marge would have attached no importance to the incident, but following as it did, the absolute lack of men other than her uncle on the spread, she wondered where they'd come from and where they were going. The more imaginative and impulsive Sally at once suspected a raid by the hooded men of the

Night Legion. Marge laughed these fears down, but she herself felt slightly apprehensive.

They climbed back into bed, drew the blankets to their chins, for the night air was getting steadily cooler, and tried hard to sleep. The lack of sounds now, seemed worse than the muttering of the men and the clump of hoofs. Both girls lay quiet, but each knew the other was wide-awake, tense, and listening for something, they knew not what. Then another sound fell on their listening ears. It seemed to come from a great distance, and yet it was clearly audible and soft. Not the sort of sound that carries far. The first time they heard it neither girl moved, then it was repeated, and Sally sat bolt upright in the darkness. Marge followed suit. It was an unmistakable sound . . . the groaning of a man in mortal anguish.

There was silence for perhaps ten minutes, when the groaning began again! It *was* a man, somewhere not far distant. His voice was weak and the groan seemed to be one of pain and utter despair. Sally wanted to leave the room, to tiptoe through the house and try to locate the sound. Marge voted against it. "Whatever it is," she told her sister, "Uncle Grant will take care of it. It's probably nothing but one of the men in the bunkhouse with a tummy ache or a toothache."

She didn't believe this herself, and she knew Sally didn't either, despite the fact that Sally agreed with her. The girls tried to tell themselves that everything was quite all right, but they felt more uneasy, apprehensive, bewildered by the ranch, with every new development.

The groaning faded off in the distance, and it seemed like hours that Marge and Sally listened for it to start again. Then finally they fell asleep.

Their first day on the ranch was half spent when they wakened. It was well past noon of the day the Lone Ranger and Tonto rode to the clearing in the woods where they met and escaped from Sheriff Cook's posse.

Natacha wakened them, explaining that Grant Whitcomb had ridden away with his men on range affairs and would probably be gone all day.

"Then I'm going to do some exploring," exulted Sally. A sense of freedom crept into both girls with the news that their uncle was not around. They bathed and dressed, and then did full justice to a belated breakfast of ham and eggs, crisp golden toast made from huge slabs of homemade bread, wild-strawberry jam, and fragrant coffee with cream thick enough to be handled with a fork. Natacha served them, and beamed at the way her cooking was appreciated. Despite her hag-like appearance, the old Indian woman proved quite likable.

Sally bolted her food, anxious to get out-of-doors and look about the place, but she was doomed to disappointment. Grant Whitcomb, when he left, made certain the girls would be secure, by posting three men as guards with strict orders to keep the girls indoors.

Sally fumed and raged, she tried acting coy and

flirtatious, she appealed to the men's chivalry, she argued for the best part of an hour, but Grant Whitcomb's men carried out his orders to the letter. The men were sorry, but orders were orders.

"What does he mean by keeping us prisoners?" demanded the quick-tempered girl. "He can't do this! How long are we supposed to stay cooped up in here?"

"Dunno ma'am," was the reply to this and all her other questions. The best Sally could achieve was a sort of explanation that it was for their good that the girls were kept indoors.

"It's because of the Night Legion," consoled Marge, when Sally finally gave up.

"Well, it's nice to know that Uncle Grant thinks so much of us, but I'd a darned sight sooner have a little more risk and more freedom."

To pass the afternoon, the girls browsed through the many books in the well-stocked library, they chatted for a time with old Natacha, and then Sally had another thought. She headed for the room where there was a trap door in the floor. "Be fun to try and open it and see what's down below," she told her sister.

But here again, Sally was frustrated. The door of the room was tightly locked, and in response to Sally's requests for the key, Natacha simply shook her head. The old crone seemed to want to tell the girls a few things, in fact, she started three times on some sort of explanation, but each time she stopped herself.

Supper came and went, with another splendidly prepared meal, but no sign of Grant Whitcomb. Then after supper a strange thing happened. Something that made the girls wonder, and gave them food for conjecture and discussion for the entire evening. It started when Sally strolled into the huge kitchen where Natacha was washing dishes. Sally chatted idly for a time, but Natacha paid her scant attention.

Then, with unusual care, and a queer look at Sally, Natacha drew a mug from the big dishpan of sudsy water. She held it for Sally to see, and pointed to the girl. "You drink-um from it," she stated.

"Sure I did, what's the matter with it?"

Natacha shook her head. "Nothin'!" She swished the water around in the pan, deep in thought. Marge entered the kitchen at that moment. Natacha saw her, and drew a mate to the mug from the water, holding it up. She pointed a lean bony finger at Marge. "Her drinkum."

Marge looked at Natacha, then at Sally, questioningly. Sally gestured silence while Natacha put the mug beside the first. She brought a third mug from the water, pointing to herself. "Me drinkum," she said, and soused the mug in rinsing water, then placed it upside down to drain. Her voice softened to a throaty guttural tone. "Uncle not here," she almost growled, "but take-um look!" A fourth mug came from the water.

"Well, who drinkum from that," demanded Sally.

The Indian shook her head slowly. "Me not tell-um!"

"Was it one of the guards outside?" asked Marge.

"Nope!"

"Then who?"

"Not tell-um."

Natacha would say no more. The girls pondered her actions for the balance of the evening. Obviously, the woman wanted the girls to realize that someone else was in the house. She had perhaps been put under oath not to reveal anything but wanted the girls to know they were not alone here. When the girls retired they were in anything but a peaceful state of mind. For lack of a better place, Marge still kept her part of the map in the toe of her boot. She was becoming increasingly glad Sally had lied about it as she had, and she was determined to keep it concealed from her uncle as long as possible, or at least until she had more trust in him than she felt at the present time. Marge wondered if when he returned Grant Whitcomb would demand the map, and failing to see it, start a thorough search, or if he'd let the matter drop with Sally's story that it was misplaced.

The breeze rustled the window curtains, and the distant sound of prairie animals harmonized with the close sound of crickets to make a restful lullaby.

Sally was muttering sleepily, as if she were thinking out loud. "Tell you one thing," she said, "I'm going to get out of this house tomorrow by hook or crook. They'll not keep me a prisoner here." She paused for several moments, then Marge heard her drowsy voice again, "Get a horse an' saddle somehow . . . . goin' to ride for Showdown, have a talk with the Sheriff there . . . " again she paused, and when she spoke her voice was softer, drowsier than ever. "Find out about the masked man . . . see what's known about Joe Frisby . . . gotta get to Showdown, lots to talk about . . . goin' t'get there, somehow . . . . " And her voice trailed off as she slept.

Neither of the girls wakened that night. They didn't know that once, a couple of hours after they'd retired, their door was softly opened and old Natacha looked in, grinned toothlessly, then closed the door as softly as she'd opened it. They didn't know that the crone crossed the narrow hall, and pulling a key from beneath her faded, many colored skirt, opened the door to the room with the iron ring in the floor. Neither did they hear Natacha leave the room a half hour later, nor did they hear Grant Whitcomb enter the big house and go to his room at three A. M. The mysterious groans of the previous night were renewed intermittently, but neither of the sisters heard them.

They slept soundly that night, while miles away across the plains, the Lone Ranger and Tonto huddled by their small campfire and discussed the note the masked man had been given by Sheriff Cook.

Marge wakened suddenly when the voice of Grant Whitcomb bellowed through the house in a tone that fairly shook the rafters. She sat up, blinked the sleep from her eyes and saw that it was daylight, but how long past sunrise she had no idea. There was something wrong! Something right in that room was not exactly as it should be. She knew! Sally was gone!

She recalled the younger girl's vows of the night before, to get out of the house, by hook or by crook. Then the door burst open and Natacha stood there waving her arms and jabbering incoherently. Grant Whitcomb's shouts, somewhere else in the house, told Marge what the Indian couldn't tell.

"Get her up," he roared. "Yuh hear me? Get Marge up an' out of there an' bring her here!"

Marge was out of bed, pulling on her clothes with frantic haste. Natacha tried to help her, jabbering all the while.

"Hurry up, in there, it's after nine o'clock an' the hoss has been gone for four hours. You Margy, d'you hear me?"

"I'm coming, Uncle," she cried. "Just a moment."

"Make it half a minute! Things have happened!"

"What has happened?" Marge had to yell to make herself heard above Natacha's voice.

"It's yer sister," came back the shout. "She sneaked away from here, takin' a hoss with her, an' she's met with a bad accident!"

Marge Whitcomb's worst fears were realized. Sally had wakened at daybreak and true to her word, slipped from the house to the saddle shed, then to the corral, and when she rode away, one of two things must have happened. Either the wild western horse she'd selected had thrown her for a nasty spill, with almost any injury a possibility, or she had fallen into the hands of the Night Legion.

She felt an awful emptiness in the pit of her stomach. It was minutes before the girl regained enough composure to call out, "What happened to Sally?"

"Don't know for sure yet. One of the men found her, but git out here an' come on with us, we'll take you to her!"

Marge was finally dressed. She hurriedly knotted her hair and pulled on her shoes . . . . feeling as she did so, the tightly folded bit of paper that still nested in the toe of one. Then she grabbed a jacket from a peg near the door and hurried to her uncle's side. "I—I'm ready, Uncle Grant," she stammered.

" 'Bout time," was the sharp reply. "Come on." Seizing the girl's hand, the big man fairly dragged her through the front door of the house. Men were in evidence near the corral, tossing saddles on the dodging horses. One of them came toward Grant Whitcomb on the run. Marge thought she'd never seen an uglier, more repulsive face on any man, than on the one who came to meet them. One side of his evil greasy-looking face was drawn up by a badly healed scar and his broken nose seemed to spread halfway across his cheek. "Boss, BOSS," he screamed at Grant Whitcomb, "someone has robbed me."

"What are you talkin' about, Scar?" bellowed Whitcomb.

"It's my vest, the blue one with the glass buttons!"

"I can't bother about that now! We got more important things to tend to!"

"I left it in the saddle shed, an' it's been stolen!"

"Find it later," snapped Whitcomb, and then to Marge, "come on, we'll get them hosses an' start out right away!"

The whole thing was a grim nightmare to Marge. She moved as in a dream, not knowing where she was about to be led, or what she'd find at the end of the trail. She firmly believed that Sally had met with some sort of tragic circumstance and she could imagine the small girl, so full of the joy of living, now crushed and broken, calling for her sister. Marge choked back a sob, determined to keep her chin up and her head level, as she knew Sally would do in the same situation. When she and Grant Whitcomb rode away from the vicinity of the house, several other men rode with them, but Marge didn't even know the direction in which they were riding. Her mind was filled with thoughts of Sally.

CHAPTER XVI

The Blue Silk Vest

"Sheriff," drawled the deputy from Texas, "I've heard considerable about this yere Lone Ranger that took the notion to call on you last evenin' at yore house."

"I reckon," replied Sheriff Cook as he watched the poker face of Tex Wilson for a sign of his personal opinion of the Lone Ranger, "I reckon they's plenty that you ain't heard, too."

"Mebbe so."

"As for his bein' in cahoots with the Night Legion, that's a lot of foolishness. He ain't no more one of them killers than I am, *and*," he added emphatically, "I'm darned sure I ain't!"

Walrus tilted his chair back against his favorite wall of the Sheriff's office, and expectorated at his favorite cuspidor. Dave Sands occupied himself with an intent survey of his close-trimmed finger nails.

Tex Wilson had been standing, but now he moved close to the Sheriff's desk, sat partly on its edge and swung one foot clear of the floor. He shoved his broad brimmed hat back further on his head and spoke slowly and softly. "I crave to know jest why you gave the masked man that evidence that sent us to the clearin' after him yisterday."

Sheriff Cook frowned darkly at the young, broad-shouldered deputy. He was not used to being spoken to like this, and he resented it. "Fer the newest of the deputies," he said, "you're takin' a lot on yourself, questionin' what I do."

"I come all the way from Texas tuh corral some of them hooded rats! I don't know if this masked man around here is the *real* Lone Ranger or not. Do you?"

Cook nodded that he did. "I seen him ridin' away on that white stallion. That's all I needed tuh convince me."

It was the morning after the masked rider called on the Sheriff, and the four men were meeting in the usual place, the Sheriff's office, while they awaited the arrival of Joe Frisby's body. Men had started out to fetch it back for decent burial, and it seemed the best plan to wait until it came, before making any other move. In fact, though all four men were eager to fight the Night Legion, they had no idea where to begin. No one had! The Night Legion couldn't be hunted in any particular place. They seemed to ride from nowhere, strike, ravage and destroy and kill, then disappear.

Walrus started the talk about the Lone Ranger, and Tex Wilson, a trifle suspicious, took the matter up with Sheriff Cook. "I'm overlookin' your manner," the Sheriff told the Texan, "fer one pertickler reason. I feel that you're as eager tuh see these killers killed off as I am, an' yuh don't miss a chance tuh look intuh anything that don't sound straight to you."

"That's jest what I aim tuh do, Sheriff," replied the other, somewhat milder than before. "If you could jest be dead sure yuh seen the real Lone Ranger an' not an imitation . . ."

"I am dead sure."

"Gosh, it's most too much tuh expect, tuh have *him* around here."

"Yuh see, Tex," the lawman went on softly, "any darn fool can figger he is doin' all that can be done, an' go ahead with his authority, bullheaded-like. It takes somethin' of a man tuh admit that, in spite of his authority, they might be someone that could do a better job than he's doin'. It likewise takes a good man tuh admit he's buckin' ag'in somethin' that's too big fer him tuh handle. Mebbe I ain't as big a man as I'd like tuh be, but by darn, I'm big enough tuh admit that the Lone Ranger can do more than all of us put tuhgether can. That's why I gave him that paper when he wanted it! What's more, he can have anything else I got, for the askin', an' if he wants it, HE CAN HAVE MY BADGE AN' OFFICE!"

"SO THERE!" finished Walrus, punctuating his speech with another bull's-eye in the spittoon!

"Miss an' yuh clean it up," growled the Sheriff at the old man. "This outfit," he continued, "is goin' tuh be brought intuh this office, held fer trial, tried, convicted an' hanged! I'll do it, if I have tuh deputize the hull blamed state tuh do it!" He brought his

clenched fist down on his desk with a slam that made
the inkstand jump and ink slop over on the oak top.
"If the leader of the Night Legion was my own brother, it wouldn't matter none. *He's got tuh die!*"
He rose to his feet, suddenly, and with his heel shoved
back his chair. His voice was trembling with the
passion of his hatred for the marauders. "What's
more, I'm dishin' up new orders here an' now! The
army can't help us, they're too busy fightin' Injuns,
so it's up to us! When yuh see a man in a hood,
don't take the chance of tryin' tuh fetch him in alive.
Shoot on sight!"

Walrus was nodding his head vigorously, delighted
with his friend's commands.

"What's more, don't shoot for legs or arms. When
yuh shoot, shoot tuh kill!"

"That's the talk!" applauded Walrus. "That's the
way tuh deal with them skunks! By thunder, Sheriff,
yore the best gol-blasted lawman in the state. The
best in the country!" he corrected. Then he went even
further, "The best, by damn, in the world." The en-
thusiasm of the old-timer was unbounded. "The man
that says yuh ain't, can fight it out with me!" With
that he glared at Tex and then at the silent Dave
Sands, as if he defied them to question his statement.

Tex Wilson grinned at the fervor in the old man's
voice and expression. Then he turned again to face
the Sheriff. "Jest wanted tuh make sure of where you
stood," he explained. "I sure as thunder hope you
don't take no offense at the things I said. It's doggone

good tuh feel dead-sure of yuh, as I do now." He
stuck out his hand toward Sheriff Cook.

Cook gripped the Texan's hand tightly and nodded.
His intended reply was interrupted by Dave Sands.
"Wagon comin' down the road. They're likely bring-
in' the remains of old Joe Frisby in."

The four men left the office to see the buckboard,
drawn by a pair of grays, approaching ahead of a
dense cloud of billowing dust. One of the two men on
the seat waved a greeting while the other drew the
team up alongside the quartette of lawmen. "Got
ᵗhe old feller with us," the driver said, pointing with
his thumb to a blanket-wrapped bundle on the buckboard.

"Good enough," replied Sheriff Cook. "We'll see to
it that the poor old crittur gets a decent Christian
burial. That's the least we c'n do for him." He gave
the necessary orders to have the body taken care of
by some of the townsmen who came up out of curiosity. For several minutes everyone was occupied
with final attentions to Joe Frisby, and no one noticed
the approach of the rider who reined up on the fringe
of the small crowd.

Sally Whitcomb's blonde hair poked out in rebel
curls from beneath the big sombrero she wore. Her
flannel shirt was open at the throat and the sleeves
were rolled up above the elbows. Her slender arms
were well-tanned from outdoor recreation in the east
and her hands were covered by fawn-colored gloves.
Her pert nose was shiny from the long ride. All of

these details, however, escaped old Walrus who was
the first of the men to see the girl.

His mouth hung open, as if no words could be found
to fit the occasion. He stared wide-eyed at the man's
blue vest she'd put on over the shirt, and the overalls
that were many sizes too large for her, and had to be
rolled up several folds at the bottom. For lack of
words, Walrus nudged his friends and pointed. They
turned to meet the level gaze of the blue-eyed girl.
"M-m-my gosh!" stammered Walrus finally. "She ...
she's a GIRL, an' wearin' men's clo'es!"

"What if I am," snapped Sally in reply. "Stop
ogling me and tell me where to find the Sheriff."

"I—I ain't doin' that ma'am," faltered the dumb-
founded deputy. "I—I was only lookin' at that git-up
yore wearin'!"

"That's my business! These clothes are easier to
ride in than a divided skirt, and I borrowed them
from men at my uncle's ranch. Now if that satisfies
your curiosity, tell me where to find the Sheriff, and
close your mouth before you catch some flies in it!"

Sheriff Cook stepped toward the girl and lifted a
hand to aid her in dismounting. She saw the star
pinned to his vest, understood that he was the man
she sought, and accepted his hand to swing from her
horse in boyish fashion and drop lightly to the ground.

Dave Sands, looking at Sally Whitcomb, was re-
warded with a slight trace of a smile and for the first
time for as long as he could remember, he felt jarred
and confused. He wanted to speak but his tongue

seemed to cling to the roof of his mouth. He knew he was blushing and he hated himself for it!

"Better step inside the office," suggested the Sheriff. "I'm afeared men around here ain't used tuh seein' —" he paused in time to avoid saying what he'd intended to, "to seein' handsome girls," he finished rather lamely.

"And in men's pants!" blurted Walrus. Then he wondered why Dave Sands jabbed him hard in the ribs with an elbow.

"Guess you must be one of Whitcomb's nieces that come on the stage, ain't you?"

Sally told the Sheriff that she was, and that her name was Sally. Five minutes later the Sheriff, Sally, and the three deputies were inside the office, with the windows crowded with men trying to see inside, and the girl felt quite at home and at ease.

She enjoyed the sensation she created, and took special delight in asking Dave Sands direct questions, just to see him squirm and stammer in his efforts to reply. When Sally was helping Sheriff Cook to spell her name, her sister's name, the place they came from and several other details, Dave found the chance to whisper to Tex Wilson. "I never knowed they growed that sort of girls exceptin' in the picture magazines that we see once in a while."

"Your type of girl all right," agreed Tex Wilson.

"Don't you like her style?" asked Dave in genuine surprise.

"Sure, I like her well enough, but I'd a darn sight

sooner fall fer a girl that's more quiet an' . . . well more dignified."

Dave bristled a bit at this. "Don't you say nothin' ag'in Miss Sally."

Tex chuckled softly to end the bit of conversation. He hoped the girl would care something for his friend. There was no doubt that as far as Dave was concerned, it was already a case of love.

Meanwhile, with the two young deputies talking to each other, and Walrus still somewhat awe-struck at beauty and charm in a place like Showdown, Sally told Sheriff Cook why she had come to town. She explained the calling of the ranch a Hoodoo Ranch by a man in Gila Gap. She told of her uncle's strange manner of receiving her and her sister, and of the groans heard during the first night on the ranch.

The Sheriff was a sympathetic listener. Sally found it increasingly easy to confide in him, and when she learned that the masked man who'd escorted her and Marge to the ranch was well thought of by the Sheriff, she was convinced that Cook was just as fair-minded and honest as his stern face indicated. His opinion of the Lone Ranger paralleled that of Sally and her sister.

"What I really wanted to come here for, was to tell you about the map."

"What map?" inquired Sheriff Cook.

Sally told him, explaining how the part owned by the girls was concealed and how she'd withheld it from her Uncle Grant. She told how the other half was owned by Joe Frisby until the Night Legion killers stole it.

Mention of the Night Legion brought Tex, Dave and Walrus closer with marked attention.

"That explains why Joe was killed," decided the sheriff.

"That's what the masked man . . . . you called him, 'The Lone Ranger' said."

"You made a mistake, though, in mistrustin' yore uncle, Miss Sally. Grant Whitcomb is as square a man as there is to be found any place. I'd vouch fer him under any an' all conditions. I'll admit he's a peculiar actin' crittur, an' he sometimes seems downright bitter about life in general, but he's on the level."

"I still think he had no business keeping us locked in the house, and guarded by men with guns."

"It was fer yer own good that he done it. Now get this straight, an' remember I'm not talkin' just to cause you girls a pack of worry. This Night Legion has already got more cash than they c'n ever spend. They don't rob an' kill an' plunder just tuh git cash. They do it *fer the love of it!*" Cook paused to let his warning register before he continued. "Them snakes would as soon kill a poor man as a rich one, and they'd likely prefer killin' a couple girls like you, than men! Now you get back to the ranch, I'll send a couple of men to see you there safe an' sound."

"I'll go," volunteered Dave Sands with alacrity. Sheriff Cook's eyes twinkled slightly and he nodded acceptance of the eagerly made offer.

"Get back there, tell your sister to turn that map over to yer uncle an' take orders from him! There ain't but a few men in the world I'm dead certain are on the level, outside the ones in this office. One of them is the Lone Ranger, and the other is your Uncle Grant."

"W-well .. all right then." Sally was loathe to believe the best of Uncle Grant, despite the sheriff's recommendation. If she knew that at that very moment, her sister was riding with the strange-acting man, as a result of a direct lie . . . but she didn't know.

Perhaps if Sheriff Cook had known that early the same morning, Grant Whitcomb had gone to Marge and told her that Sally was in trouble and needed her badly, while in truth, Sally was *not* in trouble and did *not* need her sister, he, too, might have thought a long time before advising the blonde girl, in the blue vest with glass buttons, to return to the ranch and trust Grant Whitcomb implicitly.

"I—I suppose there's nothing for me to do, but go back there then," finally admitted Sally.

"You go back, an' tell yer uncle that we're doin' all we can tuh get a lead on the Night Legion. Tell him we got the Lone Ranger on our side. I'll bet he's heard of the Lone Ranger, even if he don't get far from his ranch!"

Then a door at the rear of the office opened suddenly, and a tall man, whose face was concealed by a black mask, entered the room with one hand near the ivory handle of a heavy gun. Three of the lawmen reached for guns, but the sharp voice of Sheriff Cook halted the gesture. "Hold it, boys!"

Sally turned quickly, saw the mask and burst out in almost a shout. "The Lone Ranger."

"Tonto rode fast to bring me the news that has been flying around the town." The masked man's voice was slightly breathless from hard riding. "He said there was a girl here, wearing a blue silk vest!"

"An' overalls!" supplied old Walrus.

"A vest," the deep-voiced man went on, "with fancy glass buttons." He strode directly to the girl's side, and grabbed a handful of the vest she wore unbuttoned.

"Wha .. what's the matter with this vest?"

"Here's where there's a button torn off!" He stuck his long, lean fingers in a pocket of his shirt and drew out a glass button with a fancy trimming around the edge. "This is a button we found in the woods. It matches the buttons on that vest!"

There was a dramatic pause following the announcement. For a time none of the men grasped the full importance of the masked man's words.

"Where in the woods did you find the button?" inquired Tex Wilson.

Ignoring the question, the masked man dropped a verbal bombshell in the office. "The vest was worn by one of the men who killed Joe Frisby. *Where did you get that vest?*"

CHAPTER XVII

THE LAW STEPS IN

"You know perfectly well how much trouble I had riding to Uncle Grant's place with my own clothes. They weren't at all suited for riding!"

The Lone Ranger nodded. "The vest," he prompted, trying to reach the point quickly.

"I'm telling you about it!" Sally wouldn't be hurried in her recital of details. "I sneaked out of the house at daybreak, because I wanted to get to town as soon as possible, and had to slip away from guards to do it. I went to the saddle shed, to get a saddle for one of the horses, and found some clothing hanging on the wall . . . on pegs. This vest was 'way too big for me, but it was shorter than my jacket, so I left the jacket there and wore the vest. The same with—" she paused, glanced at the overalls, then glanced somewhat defiantly at the steely grey eyes that watched her from behind the slits in the mask.

"Do you know whose vest it is?"

"Nope. It must belong to one of the cowboys at Uncle Grant's place."

"Grant Whitcomb will shoot him down," observed the sheriff, "if he suspects he's lined up with the Night Legion."

"I wonder if he will," murmured the masked man. It was mostly luck that made it possible for him to be there. His original plans to ride that morning for the Whitcomb ranch were changed when he and Tonto met Sally Whitcomb riding in the opposite direction. The girl hadn't seen the two but she passed within a hundred feet of the rocks behind which they crouched while she went by. Tonto followed her to town and mingled with the townsmen when the buckboard brought Joe Frisby's body in. Then when the Indian got a close-up view of Sally, he rushed back to where the masked man waited. The Lone Ranger lost no time in getting to the office of the sheriff to inspect the blue silk vest.

"If this vest belongs to one of the Night Legion, then I'd certainly like to find the owner!"

Sally told the Lone Ranger in as few words as possible, the things she had already told in detail to the sheriff.

Then Dave Sands stepped forward. "Miss Sally," he began slowly, "from the things that've come up, it looks like the ranch ain't as safe as we thought it might be. If the owner of that vest has missed it, an' thinks you might be able tuh tell whose it was, he'll likely try to dry gulch you on the way back. Now if you'd stay here in town, the rest of us could head for the ranch—"

"Not on your life," declared the vivacious girl, "I'm going along with you, and see the fun!"

"Ain't goin' tuh be no fun, ma'am," argued Dave.

"Whatever it is, I'm going with you. My sister is there, you know."

"But," interposed Tex Wilson, "yore sister ain't wearin' a vest that might belong tuh one o' them killers."

"I'm going with you just the same!" The manner in which Sally Whitcomb made her decision left no room for argument. "And," she said, "what's more, you might lend me a gun and show me how to use it so I can take part in the gun play."

"Gosh," breathed Dave Sands, "what a girl."

"You don't git no gun," declared Tex Wilson.

"But after all, if it wasn't for me wearing this vest, you'd never have had a clue. Why should you men go and risk your lives, without letting me share the risk? I've decided to go with you, so that part is settled. Now don't send a girl among a group of hard men, any one of whom might be a member of the Night Legion, without a weapon to defend herself!" She looked archly at Dave Sands. "You wouldn't let me go there defenseless, would you . . . D—Dave?" She softened her voice and looked at the young deputy in a way that did things to him.

"You ain't a-goin," he muttered.

"What's that?" The others were watching the discussion which seemed to have centered on Dave and Sally.

"I said you wasn't goin'." Dave spoke more firmly than before. "Tain't good sense tuh let a kid like you risk yer life."

"Kid!" cried Sally. "I like *that!*"

"Yuh ain't goin' an' that settles it!" Dave seemed to have made up his mind quite definitely on the subject. "You ain't goin' tuh that ranch until we get there an' look around some!"

"You just try and stop me," challenged the girl.

"Yes'm," Dave took half a step forward, hesitated as the slender girl stood firm. "I—I reckon I'll have tuh do that very thing." He took another step, and grabbed Sally around the waist, then picked her off the ground. Sally squealed, kicked, squirmed, and struggled. She tried to slap the stalwart deputy in the face, she tried to pinch his muscled arm, and knocking off his hat, she gripped his dark hair in both hands and pulled with all her strength, but nothing stopped Dave Sands.

He carried her bodily through the small barred door at the end of the sheriff's office.

"You can't do this, you big bully," screamed Sally. "What's the matter with the rest of you men! Won't any of you help me?"

She appealed to the others collectively, then individually, but none of the others made a move to interfere with Dave Sand's plan to lock her in the prison. "You can't jail me, I'm not a criminal, I'll—" she ended in a grunt as Dave Sands dropped her on the bunk, then she leaped to her feet and raced for the door, just as the deputy slammed it in her face and locked it!

"Thar," he said, wiping his perspiring face with his bandanna.

"I reckon that'll keep yuh safe fer a time. I don't aim tuh let no killers get at *my* girl!"

Sally was desperately angry. She never before had been shown so little consideration. Used to having her own way with men, she found a new type of people in the West. A type upon which her usual methods of persuasion had little effect.

"Y—you . . . your girl!" she sputtered in rage. "Of all the bare-faced nerve, of all the overgrown, mean, cruel bullies, you take the prize! I'd sooner die than be your girl. You who picks on defenseless women!"

"Defenseless," chuckled Walrus, "my eye!" He looked at Dave Sands' perspiring face, the red welts on his cheek where Sally's open hand had landed with a hard slap, and the tousled hair that fell over the deputy's forehead. "That gal has what I'd call a doggone good defense!"

The Lone Ranger agreed to Sheriff Cook's suggestion that he travel with them to Grant Whitcomb's place. "If we start now we can be there in time to give us the chance to look around in daylight."

"Very well," responded the masked man.

"What about yer Indian friend?"

"Tonto will remain here in town. Sally Whitcomb will be held here, and it's possible that someone might make an attempt to kill her. I'll feel that she is much safer if my friend is close at hand."

This was agreeable to Sheriff Cook, so the masked man went to the rear door of the building, wrote a few hasty words on a page torn from a small notebook he carried, and tucked the message into a small crack between the door casing and the wall of the building. Tonto, he know, would be watching from a distance, and would read the note and obey the commands.

When he returned, the Lone Ranger found Sally Whitcomb very much subdued. Her anger seemed to have died down to be replaced by tears. Whether the girl was really crying, or putting on an act, he couldn't decide, but he saw Dave Sands squirming uncomfortably, feeling like a criminal because of the way he'd handled the slight girl with the curly blonde hair.

Sally sobbed "D—Dave," and when the deputy sheriff looked at her, she motioned for him to come nearer to the barred door of the cell. "I-I wa-want to s-s-speak to you," she whimpered.

"Yes'm?"

"Y-you're cruel," Sally sobbed.

"Aw-w-w gosh, Miss Sally, I-I hated like blazes tuh have tuh put yuh in there, but it's fer yer own good. I don't want yuh bein' shot tuh death, no more'n yer Uncle Grant does."

"B-but when I was held a prisoner all day yesterday, I wasn't left alone. I had Marge, my sister, to keep me company. I-I d-don't want to stay here all alone."

"But you're goin' tuh be watched, Miss Sally, the Indian named Tonto is goin' tuh see tuh that."

"B-but can't you stay here? You don't have to ride to the ranch with the others, do you?"

Dave would have given a lot to be able to remain with the attractive girl. He was head over heels in love with her already and he'd known her only half an hour. He glanced at Sheriff Cook inquiringly. Cook shook his head. "You're goin' with us," he stated. "That girl is aimin' tuh be left alone with you an' ten minutes after we're gone, she'll have you unlockin' that door an' she'll be on her way tuh the ranch."

Dave looked at Sally and gestured to show the hopelessness of trying to remain behind when the others left. In a few moments Sally was alone in the building. She heard the men mount horses and ride away. Then she half grinned and said to herself, "Dave is mighty nice, and I think he likes me. Hope nothing happens to him!"

It would take at least two hours of steady loping to reach Grant Whitcomb's ranch, so the five men settled down in their saddles for the trip. The Lone Ranger rode beside the sheriff, making plans for a systematic investigation of the place when they arrived there. He told about the print he'd seen in the clearing, and Cook suggested that while he asked routine questions of Grant Whitcomb, the Lone Ranger could move about the saddle shed and hunt for a print to match the one of the boss. "Think you'll be able to recognize it?" he inquired.

The Lone Ranger nodded. "I wouldn't forget that print if it took ten years to find another like it."

"Good." For a time they rode in silence with Tex,

Walrus and Dave Sands bringing up the rear. "I
don't know," said Sheriff Cook finally, "what we'll
say about that mask of yours."

"I'm not going to remove it."

"It's all right with me, Partner, but what sort of
explanation can we give Grant Whitcomb?"

"Why give him an explanation?"

"Right now, with the Night Legion raisin' cain
around this part of the country, Whitcomb ain't the
sort to take a masked man without askin' questions."

"Why?"

"Well, in the first place, he may not have heard of
the Lone Ranger. If I tell him you're the Lone Ranger,
it mightn't tell him a blamed thing, if he ain't heard
of yuh. He'll wonder why yuh travel with lawmen,
an' keep yer face covered."

"Suppose we wait until we see him. When he asks
questions, I will answer them."

"All right, then, you answer 'em."

After leaving Showdown the riders headed due east
for a time, following the stage trail. They paused
when they came to the scene of the shooting of the
deputies and guard and driver. Dismounting, the
Lone Ranger scrutinized the ground with infinite attention to details, but it was so beaten down
that no one foot-print could be made out clearly. He
saw that a lot of men had been there, but found no
trace of the peculiar boot whose print was stamped
indelibly in his mind. The horses took advantage of
the pause to drink from a small brook that ran near

by, and then the party continued on its way. They cut northeast, to meet the trail over which the Lone Ranger and Tonto rode with the Whitcomb sisters, then followed this trail due north toward the Whitcomb ranch.

Tex Wilson and old Walrus were highly amused by the manner of Dave Sands throughout the ride. The dark-haired deputy was silent for the most part, but when he spoke it was invariably to make some comment on Sally.

"I reckon," observed the blond Tex Wilson, "that it must be true that opposites attract. Now me, I ain't nothin' tuh say against the girl, but I don't cotton much tuh light-haired women. If she jest had a sister . . ."

"But she has," said Dave emphatically.

"I mean one with dark hair. I like a quiet sort of girl, and if I could find me one with dark hair, an' a handsome face, I'd be downright interested."

Walrus shifted his tobacco to the other cheek, expectorated at a clump of greasewood. "As fer me," he stated flatly, "I don't care fer face or the color o' their hair. Gimme a woman that c'n cook!"

CHAPTER XVIII

In the Hands of the Killers

Marge had no thought that her uncle lied when he told her Sally was in dire distress and needed her. Without a moment's hesitation, she mounted the horse that was saddled and ready for her at the corral and rode with Grant Whitcomb and the other men. It wasn't until a half hour after they started that she began to feel uneasy. The country was becoming steadily more desolate and broken. Rank weeds and other vegetation grew knee high over most of the hilly land as far as the eye could see, and flies and insects of a dozen sorts buzzed angrily about the riders' heads and faces. The horses, too, were bothered by the biting varieties.

To all her questions, Grant Whitcomb gave Marge unsatisfactory replies. When several of his responses were contradictory to things he'd told her earlier, her apprehension increased. It didn't seem possible that Sally would have ridden alone as far as this. If she had done so, how could Grant Whitcomb have received word of any difficulty she might have met as soon as he did.

They rode for another hour, and by that time Marge was really frightened. Sally couldn't possibly have covered that distance in the time she'd left the house. Though Marge had no idea what time Sally had left, she felt it couldn't have been much before daybreak. It was impossible for her to have ridden to this God-forsaken looking country due west of the ranch. No sign of any life, either human or animal had been seen since leaving the rambling ranch house. The men who followed behind Marge and Grant Whitcomb, spoke but rarely, and then in terse, short-clipped mono-syllables.

Marge, of course, didn't know the truth. Whit-comb saw Sally when she left the house at dawn. He seized upon her escape as an excuse to get the dark-haired girl to ride with him on this mysterious mission.

Presently Grant Whitcomb broke a lengthy silence. "I ain't said no more about the map since the other night."

"No," replied the girl. "You haven't."

"Ain't found it yet have you?" He looked at Marge sharply. She could almost feel the penetration of his gaze.

"Sally . . . " she hesitated. "M-my sister told you it was misplaced in our luggage."

"That wasn't true."

"What do you mean?"

"Natacha went through everything you brought with you."

"She had no right to do that," said Marge somewhat hotly.

Ignoring the remark, the heavy-set man went on.

"That map wasn't in your luggage, so it must be hidden by you. What about it?"

"Well, what about it? It is our map, isn't it? Haven't we the right to do what we please with it?" She was really surprised at herself. Her justifiable anger at her uncle's manner must have given her courage to speak up in such a way.

"Maybe," said the big man slowly, "you don't trust yer uncle."

"Perhaps I don't!" Marge paused, and then continued, "Have you shown me any reason to trust you? You won't even give me a truthful answer about my sister."

"What d'ya want to know about her?"

"What happened to her? Where is she?"

"Can't tell fer sure."

"Are we honestly going where she is?"

The reply was just what Marge suspected for some time, but Whitcomb's frank admission shocked her. "No, we ain't!"

"Th-then, where are we going? Why have you brought me on this ride? What has happened to my sister?"

"Lady," the bald-headed man responded, "you're goin' to learn considerable in the next few minutes. We stop the hosses right here." He drew back on the reins, and Marge did likewise. There seemed little else she could do. The men behind rode up beside them, and the one with the scar on his face looked even more sinister than before. They were at the crest of a low hill. Far beyond them, Marge could see the edge of a woods that looked cool and inviting after the hot dusty ride. The sun was straight overhead, so it must have been just about noon. The long ride without a breakfast, the hot sun, and the nervous strain of the past hour, made Marge weak and slightly faint, and she welcomed the pause, despite the fact that grim details seemed about to be presented.

"Boss," growled the man with the Scar, "I'm still worried about my missin' vest."

"Stop worryin' about it," snarled Grant Whitcomb in a tone that Marge had never heard him use before.

"But there's cause tuh worry. I've lost one of the fancy buttons off'n it, an' I don't know where I lost it. If it's found it might serve as a clue."

"You mean to tell me," almost thundered Grant Whitcomb, "that you left a loose end that c'n be followed?" His hand jumped toward the heavy gun he wore.

"No, no," assured Scar hastily. "I ain't left no loose end. It ain't likely that button will ever be found, an' if it is, it ain't likely it'll be found where it'll cause any trouble."

"We'll see about that later. If I find you left any loose ends though—." The leader left his threat unfinished, but Scar fully understood the grim meaning the words implied.

"I wonder," muttered the scar-faced man, "if that girl found the vest an' wore it when she went to Showdown?"

"Is that where my sister went?" asked the dark-haired girl quickly.

"What if it is," barked her uncle. A peculiarly evil grin broke the corners of his small mouth. He slipped one foot from the stirrup and swung his short leg over the saddle, turning partly to the side and leaning his weight on his elbow. "Marge," he said slowly, "there's a lot you'd like to know, ain't there?"

Marge nodded, somewhat faint and confused by everything. Her uncle's sudden changes of manner baffled her.

"Well, that sort of makes us even. There's a lot you want to know, an' there's likewise a lot I want to know. I aim tuh find out the things I want to know before the day is out, an' maybe you'll do the same."

"I'm not going another inch until you tell me about my sister."

"Now that sort of actin' won't git yuh nowheres. Right over yonder at the edge of that woods is where we're goin'."

"I'm going back to the ranch," declared the girl with a fire in her voice that was more like Sally. She dragged on the reins to swing her horse, but Scar reached out with his huge hand and grabbed the reins.

"Not so fast," he muttered.

"Let go of my bridle!"

"Yore goin' with us," said Grant Whitcomb. "I fetched these boys along tuh make sure of it." He spoke sharply to Scar, "The rest of the boys will be coming tuh meet us, an' this is about as far as I hanker tuh go with my face showin'. None of the others know who the Boss is."

The scar-faced man nodded. "I'll hang on tuh the girl's hoss till yer ready, Boss."

The events of the next moment made Marge's senses reel giddily. She saw her uncle draw a black hood from beneath his shirt. He removed his hat and slipped the weird device over his bald head. It fell in loose folds on his shoulders but it fit snugly on the top of his head. He put the sombrero on over the hood and his sharp, beady eyes studied the girl through the slits in the black cloth.

Marge Whitcomb's face went chalk-white. She was vaguely aware that Scar and the other men had drawn their guns, and sat holding them easily but ready for instant use. The countless questions that had passed through Marge's mind since her arrival at the ranch were answered. The explanation for Grant Whitcomb's manner; his interest in her part of the map; the strange room with the trap door in the floor; sounds in the night; the death of Joe Frisby—all were explained in the action of Grant Whitcomb in covering his head with that sinister-looking hood. Her uncle, the man she'd traveled over a thousand miles to live with, was *the hooded leader of the dread Night Legion!*

Her uncle, a man wanted for countless crimes, but who left no loose ends . . . *no loose ends!* If he let the girl live after revealing his connection to her, he would leave a loose end, a person who could identify him for what he was! What chance had she to return from this ride alive! What chance had Sally, after the men returned to the ranch? Her brain spun crazily as the full danger of her position became more evident. An endless dizzy sequence of horrible images flashed through her mind. The men who'd been murdered; the guard and driver of the stage; the tales of torture she'd been told, and above all, her own grim peril.

Her own letters told Grant Whitcomb that Joe Frisby had half of the map, and explained the value of the bit of paper. It had been those letters which sent the hooded legion to kill Joe Frisby, and secure his map. Before he died, old Joe talked to the Lone Ranger, but the Lone Ranger, though Marge didn't know it, was at that moment in the sheriff's office at Showdown, talking to her sister Sally. The Lone Ranger, the one man who might be able to give aid, was countless miles away.

The sharp voice of the man behind the black hood broke through her racing thoughts. "Well," he snapped, "now you know what I am, what are you goin' to do about it?"

Marge couldn't reply. Stark terror seized her. She reeled a moment, then fell to one side and would have dropped to the ground, if Scar hadn't caught her. He supported her in the saddle while he asked, "Now what'll we do with her? She's fainted!"

"Carry her if yuh have to. We ain't much further tuh go now. The rest of the boys will be already waiting at the cave just beyond the edge of the woods."

"Flynn's Cave is the meetin' place, eh?"

The black hood bobbed as the leader nodded.

"D'ya think this one's got the map, or has the tow-headed girl got it?"

"I dunno, but we got ways *tuh* find out. Wait'll we get her tuh the cave. Come on." Grant Whitcomb jabbed his horse's flanks with big rowels and moved ahead. Supporting Marge on her horse between them, the other men followed in silence, both grinning slightly at what they fancied might be an amusing bit of entertainment, when they reached Flynn's Cave.

Marge regained consciousness in a few minutes, and thought at first she was waking from some fearsome nightmare, that featured spectres with black hoods on their heads. She was at first half amused at the ridiculous story of her dream. It was incredible that her Uncle Grant could be the leader of the hooded men.

Then the jouncing of her horse cleared the remaining fog away from her mind, and she saw the ugly men who held her in the saddle. And, slightly ahead, she saw the familiar broad back of Grant Whitcomb. She saw the hood and realized that this was not a dream, but grim reality. She must, she realized, keep her wits about her, if there were to be any hope for life. For a time she remained limp. She let the men think she was still unconscious to have time to think and adapt herself as far as possible to the situation at hand.

The outlaws wanted her part of the map. She was certain of this. She could feel it with her toe, inside her boot. They had already indicated that they didn't know whether she or her sister had the bit of paper on their person. As long as they weren't sure where the map was they might keep her alive, but she knew that once they had the map in their possession, there would be no point in keeping her alive. It would be too much of a hazard to let her live, because she could tell the name of the leader.

Sally's life would depend upon her. If the men were made to think her sister had the map, they'd lose no time in fetching Sally to this awful place of desolation. She had to think, she had to plan carefully. She must not for a single moment let the men think Sally had the map, and yet, she mustn't let them get it from her. Perhaps she might be able to send them on a wild goose chase to some place near the ranch. At least she'd be given a reprieve till the men sent to investigate came back empty-handed.

In taking stock of the situation, she thought once more of the Lone Ranger. There was no reason to suppose he knew of her peril. After all, it had been the masked man who brought her to her uncle's place. Yet she couldn't bring herself to believe he was in league with the Night Legion. The same sixth sense that made her doubt her uncle from the time she first saw him, made her feel that the Lone Ranger was a friend upon whom she might count. But the Lone Ranger couldn't know of Whitcomb's connection.

She risked opening her eyes a bit to look ahead. With a start she saw the hooded man gazing straight at her. "Awake, eh," he growled. Marge saw that further feigning of unconsciousness was out of the question, so she gathered her strength to sit erect.

"Y-yes," she replied to the man's questions. "I'm awake." It was hardly necessary to admit this. Grant Whitcomb had dropped back until he rode beside the others, and motioning to Scar to ride ahead, he moved close alongside Marge's paint horse. Less than a hundred yards ahead, at the edge of the woods, Marge saw a group of horses clustered at the base of a cliff that seemed about twenty-feet in height.

"You think a lot of your sister, don't you?" asked the hooded man. Marge nodded silently. "Then I'll make a deal with you. You see none of my men know who I am except these two that rode with us. Now you know it. If you so much as make a peep to tell the others you'll meet who I am, you'll do the same as sign a death warrant for your sister."

At least Sally was still unharmed. This was some comfort to the trembling girl.

"Remember that when you get inside the Cave." There was no promise of life for her but this would be more than Marge could hope for.

The ground dipped down as the horses neared the wall which was much higher than it appeared from the level stretch behind them. Marge saw the opening of a cave some eight feet in height. She had a fleeting notion to snatch the reins suddenly and make a break for her life, but she immediately discarded this as hope-less.

Her own strength was gone, and the men with her seemed as fresh as when the ride had started. Her uncle was close on one side and the other man still gripped her arm on the other. There was no escape for her. Scar, riding ahead, guided his horse inside the blackness of the cave, and then, three abreast with Marge Whitcomb in the center, the others followed. Dense darkness enveloped the girl like a shroud.

CHAPTER XIX

Dark Depths

"As long as I've knowed Grant Whitcomb I never knew him tuh do a thing that wasn't strictly on the level, and I've knowed him fer a good many years." It was Sheriff Cook who spoke. During the last mile of the trip to Whitcomb's ranch, the Lone Ranger had asked quite a number of questions.

"But why is it," inquired the masked man, "that he is so little known around the country? I find people who have lived around here just as long as he has, who have never seen him."

"He don't work like other cattle men. He hires men tuh do all his work for him. Not only the wranglin' an' herdin' an' brandin' an' all that sort of thing, but the sellin' an' everything else includin' the collectin' of cash an' bankin' that same in Showdown."

"What does he do with all his time?"

"Wal," Sheriff Cook reflected for a moment, "he does some writin' an' considerable readin'. It's said he's got more books in his house than all t'other folks in the state put tuhgether. Most every month or so, they's a case of books comes from the East fer him."

"He pays his men pretty well, doesn't he?"

"Better than anyone else around here. He demands

a lot o' his men, but he's willin' tuh pay fer it."

"What does he demand?"

"Oh, he won't let 'em head fer a drinkin' spree on pay day, an' he don't like fer them tuh mix none with the waddies from other ranches, an' he fires a man if he hears that he's took a drink—things like that." The sheriff tried to answer all the questions asked by the Lone Ranger, knowing that there was a motive in the masked man's desire for information. "I know what yer drivin' at," he stated after a pause of several minutes, broken only by the steady rhythm of the horses' hoofs. "Yuh got a notion that Grant Whitcomb is mixed up in the Night Legion but he can't be, because he was here when the Night Legion worked in Texas!"

"Just how did his place happen to be called the Hoodoo Ranch?"

"Tain't nothin' you can put yer finger on. Some addle-headed Injuns started that story, but there wasn't nothin' to it. One time when Old Walrus rode by the place he heard a man screamin' bloody murder, so he come fer me fast. We went there an' the hullabaloo wasn't nothin' but a man named Scar Fenton with a toothache an' a couple of the men was pullin' out the trouble-makin' tooth. It was all over when we got there."

"On that trip, did you see Grant Whitcomb?"

"Yere, but he was havin' eye-trouble from too much readin', so we didn't stay long. Had tuh sit in a darkened room while we talked. Thar's the ranch an' it looks sort of deserted—don't see no one around."

None of the men were visible as the riders came near. The Lone Ranger recalled the same absence of men on his previous approach to the place, but as before, he didn't attribute much importance to the fact. The Whitcomb ranch extended over thousands of acres and the men might be anywhere on that vast expanse attending to some of the innumerable chores.

They came close to the house, drew up the horses and dismounted. "Whitcomb should be inside, it's said that the sun hurts his eyes so he don't leave the house much in daylight." He hammered on the door then waited for a response. "Curious," he muttered, and hammered louder. Still no response. "Mebbe asleep, but the old Injun woman that does his cleanin' an' cookin' should be there." Slipping his gun from its sheath, the sheriff used the butt to pound on the door in a fashion that would waken the soundest sleeper. He sent Tex Wilson to investigate the rear door of the far-flung house, "Better take Dave Sands along with you," he advised. The two youthful deputies moved off.

"The door," suggested the Lone Ranger, "is probably unlocked. I'm going to walk right in." He tried the door and found he was correct. It swung open easily on well-greased hinges. With Cook and Walrus close behind him, the masked man stepped into the big living room where Marge and Sally first saw their Uncle Grant. The windows were tightly curtained and the hangings dra n together to shut out most of the late afternoon light. The house seemed cold and damp, and utterly lacking in warmth or cheer of any sort. There was a clamminess that a fire in the huge fireplace would have driven out, but no fire burned, and there were no ashes of a recent fire or no wood laid for a future one.

The Lone Ranger thought he heard a shuffling sound. He whirled quickly from the fireplace, and saw Natacha standing in the entrance of a hallway that ran back into the other part of the big building. "Natacha?" he inquired.

The wrinkle-faced old woman nodded slowly, but she didn't speak. Sheriff Cook and Walrus brushed past her with guns held ready. Something seemed to tell them that things at the house were not as they should be. Rather than waste time trying to put questions to Natacha, Cook had decided to investigate for himself. The masked man was about to follow, but a hand with fingers like the talons of a bird of prey closed on his arm. "You wait," muttered old Natacha. The Lone Ranger paused and looked at her through the slits of his mask. Her black eyes burned fiercely, directly into his. "Me show-um you," she added.

He wondered if this might be some sort of trap. He could hear the rear door open as Tex and Dave Sands were admitted by the sheriff, then he heard their voices as they divided into pairs to begin a systematic search of the place. Why had the crone singled him out as the one to confide in? He was about to leave her and join the others when she spoke again. "Other men not bother with Natacha. You mebbe listen?"

She was offended, that was it. The others hadn't bothered to seek aid from her. She'd show them by assisting the masked man that their oversight and disregard for an old woman would cost them information. "You lead and I will follow," the Lone Ranger told her.

She turned and shuffled down the hall, pausing at a door on her left. From beneath a huge apron, probably from a pocket in her skirt, she took a key and unlocked the door. She stepped inside a neatly furnished, immaculately clean bedroom, and with the toe of her moccasined foot, kicked aside a hooked rug on the floor. A trap door with an iron ring sunk into the wood was exposed to the gaze of the Lone Ranger. Pointing to the ring, Natacha said, "You lift."

Alert, wary for some sort of trap, the Lone Ranger bent and gripped the ring with one hand, keeping the other in close proximity to one of his heavy guns. He lifted and the square of wood came up on hinges. He threw it back as far as the restraining piece of cord would let it go, then looked into the opening. There was a flight of stairs going down into the blackness.

The Lone Ranger drew a gun and held it in readiness, as he peered downward, trying to penetrate the utter darkness. He heard a movement behind him and turned quickly, but it was merely Natacha removing the glass chimney of an oil lamp. She struck a match and held it to the wick. The lamp flared up smokily until the chimney was replaced, then it burned with steady brilliance. The old woman held it by the glass bowl with the handle pointing toward the masked man. "You take-um," she muttered, "go-um down stair."

Still suspecting it must be some sort of trap, but willing to take any risk that would make whatever menace the cellar held assert itself, the Lone Ranger gripped the handle of the lamp, and holding it high descended to the depths.

His high heels clumped on each step. Halfway down he paused and tried to pierce the gloom with his eyes. He saw nothing beyond the small area lighted by the lamp. Finally he reached the bottom of the stairs and saw that the ground was hard-packed earth, the surface of which was slightly moist, and slimy. Here he again paused, holding the lamp above his head. He knew that presently his vision would improve as his eyes became accustomed to the darkness, but in the meanwhile he didn't propose to be a handy target for whoever might be lurking in the cellar. He turned the wick of the lamp down slightly and placed it on the floor beside him, then moved a couple paces to his right.

While he waited for his eyes to adjust themselves, his ears were tuned to catch the slightest sound of motion. He heard a drop of water fall into what seemed like a small pool, but it was far from where he stood. He tried to determine the direction of the sound, but found this impossible. After moments that seemed like eternity, he again picked up the lamp, and holding it in his left hand while his right hand grasped his .45, he moved ahead. Cautious, lest there be some sort of pit into which he could easily drop, he felt his way with one foot, making sure it was on firm ground before shifting his weight. Step by step he progressed, holding his gun hand out in front of him. Presently his hand came in contact with an obstacle. He felt a cold and slippery surface which proved to be a stone wall, the side of the cellar. He turned to the left, keeping close to the stone wall as he went on his way, trying to see beyond the small circle of light cast by the lamp. In places there were shallow pools of water on the floor but the deepest of these was less than an inch. "Probably seeped in through the stones," he reasoned. After a couple of dozen cautious steps, he came abruptly to another wall, running at right angle to the first. He turned left and began following the second wall of the cellar, but suddenly he stopped. He thought he'd heard someone or something move. "Might have been a rat," he thought, "there must be lots of them down here." The place smelled musty and didn't seem to be used at all, not even for storage. He wondered why Natacha had sent him down here. He moved on for perhaps a moment, when the light fell on a thing that brought him to a halt. It was the figure of a man sprawled on the ground.

The Lone Ranger dropped to his knees and set the lamp down on the floor. Then, as he felt for the man's pulse, he heard another sound. It was a distant dull thud. He glanced at the stairs which had been slightly illuminated by the light from the bedroom above, but now those stairs weren't visible! He was trapped! Trapped in this cold, damp, vaultlike place just as the man on the floor beside him must have been. Natacha had tricked him neatly. That was what he thought.

His first impulse was to race across the cellar, hurry up the stairs and see if the door was locked, but he restrained himself. If the intention of Natacha was to lock it, to bar his exit from the place, she would have already done so by the time he got there. There was a flutter of life in the man whose arm he gripped and nothing could be lost by seeing if there was anything he might be able to do to aid whoever it might be.

Natacha hadn't meant to trap him. She'd heard Sheriff Cook and the deputies coming toward the room, the door of which stood open, and had closed the trap door, hurriedly covering it with the oval rug. And she was just in time. The lawmen entered the room in their systematic search.

"It's darned funny," growled the Sheriff, "where everyone has gone."

"Where's the masked man gone?" asked Tex Wilson.

"We ain't seen him since we came into the house either," added Dave Sands. "This place jest ain't right, somehow!"

"His hoss is still outside," said Walrus. "He cain't be far away."

"Is the hoss tethered?" asked Tex Wilson. Walrus

shook his head slowly that it was not. "Then the masked man ain't far from here. Knowin' that hoss as I do, it wouldn't hang around here if its master wasn't right close by."

The sheriff moved to face Natacha squarely. "You savvy English?" he asked. The woman nodded. "Then where is Grant Whitcomb at?" She signified she didn't know. "He rid away from here?" Again the crone shook her old head slowly. "Me not know-um."

"They ain't," growled Walrus as he whittled a slab of tobacco with his knife, "no use questionin' her. She wouldn't tell the truth even if she wanted tuh. Tain't a habit with her breed." He packed the wad of brown stuff in his mouth and began chewing energetically.

In his hand the sheriff held a sheaf of papers taken from an old desk found in Whitcomb's bedroom. He paused long enough to study them while the others waited. "Whatever else he done, Grant Whitcomb sure saved his mail," he commented, noting the years-old dates on some of the missives.

"Who they from?" asked Dave Sands.

"Couple from his brother before he died, an' then the girls took up the writin'. Most of the others are from one of the girls." Feeling that he was within his rights, but disliking the job just the same, Sheriff Cook scanned hastily through letters scrawled by Sally and meticulously written by Marge. "Here's one," he observed, "where she tells about the map her Pa left an' mentions Joe Frisby." He read further. "Says she's comin' out here tuh live."

"That explains one thing," observed Tex Wilson. "It tells how the Night Legion knowed there was a map. It makes us all the more sure that one of the men that has access tuh this house is a member of the Night Legion."

"But it don't find the Lone Ranger!" The sheriff stuffed the letters in his pocket and turned quickly, determined to scour the house a second time if necessary to find the Lone Ranger. "Is he here too?" growled a voice.

The men all looked toward the speaker. Grant Whitcomb stood in the doorway of the room. "It looks," he observed with an angry glint in his small black eyes, "like I got visitors."

CHAPTER XX

THE OUTLAW ROUNDUP

Marge, in desperation sought to prolong her life as much as possible, knowing that as soon as the men in Flynn's cave had the map they sought, they'd kill her without mercy. She evaded the hooded man's questions as long as possible. Then, when the other men in the dark cavern began to stir restlessly and suggested that a branding iron might bring the information they wanted, she told the man in the hood that she had placed the map beneath the oval rug in a bedroom in the house. In that, she told the truth. She didn't add that the map had been taken from its hiding place and was at that moment in her shoe.

The Boss snarled in cursing fury at the statement. Scar offered to ride back to the house and get the map. "I c'n be there by sundown an' back here by midnight," he explained. But his offer was turned down. The Boss decided that he himself would ride back to the Whitcomb house. For the benefit of the men who didn't know his identity, he said, "I'll manage tuh sneak in an' out again without bein' seen." Then he rode away with strict orders to keep a close watch on the girl.

When Grant Whitcomb reached the house, he saw

the white horse of the Lone Ranger and the horses ridden by the lawmen. He went into the house to comment on the visit.

"Is there somethin' you gents wanted here?"

"Yes, there is, Whitcomb." Sheriff Cook did the talking. "There's a few things we'd like to talk to you about. In the first place, we got reasons for thinkin' one of your men is in cahoots with the Night Legion!"

Whitcomb's eyes went wide in astonishment. "Yuh don't say so?" he remarked. "What reason you got for thinkin' that?"

"We got tuh where some of the Night Legion met, an' found a button from a fancy vest." Cook didn't go into detail as to show the button happened to be found. "Miss Sally come to Showdown wearin' that same vest with the button missin' an' she got it from a peg in yore saddle shed. We'd like to find out who has a vest of that sort."

"I'll find out for you, and I'll consider it a personal favor, Sheriff, if you let me drill the skunk myself. If I find one of my men associated with that outfit, I'll kill him!" His voice had a ring of sincerity which wasn't feigned. He *would* kill Scar, at the first opportunity. Scar had left a loose end!

"Another thing," continued Sheriff Cook, "we ain't seen anything of the oldest of yer two nieces. Ain't she around the house?"

Grant Whitcomb's mind was working rapidly. He suspected Sally had told the lawmen all about events since her arrival at the house and reasoned the best

way to avert any suspicion in the minds of the lawmen would be frankness. "Yuh see," he said, "I
thought one of the Night Legion was hangin' around
here so I told both girls to stay inside the house an'
posted guards to keep them here. The youngest girl
though . . . sneaked out of the house before daybreak
and headed for town. Then I found out from some
of my men that the man that was around here was
the Lone Ranger, and not a member of the Night
Legion. I was glad of that, because it meant the girls
wouldn't have to stay so close to the house. I took
Marge for a little ride on hossback, startin' out this
mornin'."

"Where's she now? Did she come back with you?"

Grant Whitcomb shook his head. "Nope. We got
as far as the west boundary of my land an' she wanted
tuh stay an' watch some of the boys do brandin', so
I left her there an' come on alone."

"Yore eyes seem all right now."

"They was this mornin'." Whitcomb blinked a
couple times and rubbed his eyes with a knuckle of his
fist. "But they got to botherin' me after bein' out all
day, that's why I came back ahead of Marge." His
tongue was glib and the explanation all Sheriff Cook
could look for. He didn't have any reason to suspect
Grant Whitcomb of anything out of the way in the
first place.

"They's jest one thing more, you mentioned the
Lone Ranger a while back."

Whitcomb nodded.

"He came in here with us, but we can't find him now. Have you any idea where he might be?"

"Gosh, how would I know?"

"We hunted the house through, but ain't seen him. Is there any place that he could have gone to search that we don't know about?"

"Did you look in the saddle shed?"

"Thunder!" exploded Walrus. "That's whar he went, of course. He went tuh see if them boot marks was anywhere's around it!" The lawmen trooped from the room, while Natacha and Grant Whitcomb remained behind. At a gesture from the man, the Indian woman also left. Then the Boss quickly kicked back the hooked rug and looked on the floor. He saw no sign of any paper there. "Lied tuh me," he growled softly. He lifted the rug and shook it and looked on o'her parts of the floor, but saw no map. He turned, leaving the rug where it fell, to ask Natacha about it. At the door, he heard a creak, and then a thud! He whirled to see a man's masked face appearing in the opening. With an animal-like cry of rage and fury, Whitcomb snatched at his gun. There was a shot and flame lashed from the gun held by the Lone Ranger. The silver slammed into Grant Whitcomb's weapon with a force that sent the six-gun burtling in an arc to strike the wall six feet away. Bellowing like an angry, wounded bull, the big man wrung his stinging hand. "Make a move," commanded the masked man, "and I'll let you have the next slug where it will hurt more!" He leaped nimbly from the stairs, covering Grant Whitcomb with both guns, while the lawmen, attracted by the sound of firing, returned on the run!

"What's this mean?" yelled the sheriff.

"He's shot Grant Whitcomb," bellowed Walrus.

Whitcomb screaming in his pain and rage commanded the lawmen to open fire on the Lone Ranger. "He's the man yuh want," he howled, "he's the one that's in the Night Legion"

"Stand where you are," snapped the Lone Ranger, holding his guns leveled at the astonished lawmen. "We'll find out who is a member of the Night Legion! The man you want stands right there before you!"

"That cain't be," argued the sheriff, "he's Grant Whitcomb."

"Grant Whitcomb has been imprisoned in the cellar of this place for weeks! You'll find the real Grant Whitcomb down there right now! This man came here from Texas, heard that Whitcomb was very little known or understood, so he came here and took over the ranch. To carry out his deception he had to shave the top of his head and his eyebrows! You can see a little stubble already growing in!" Jamming one gun in a holster, the Lone Ranger advanced quickly, grabbed at the shirt of the imposter and dragged out something black! "Here," he cried exultantly. "I saw the end of this showing from beneath his shirt." He held the fabric up where all could see it, and unquestionably it tagged the big man for what he was. It was a hood, such as were worn by the Night Legion.

"A couple of you get down below and help the *real* Grant Whitcomb. He's weak and suffering from a bad cold, but proper care will make him well again!"

As he spoke, the Lone Ranger rapidly felt of the pockets of the glowering man. A slight crinkle of paper attracted his exploring fingers, and dipping into the pocket he brought out a map or rather half a map. He identified it quickly. "Did you," he snapped, "get this from Marge Whitcomb?"

"No!"

"Where did you get it?"

"It—it's mine. It . . . that is . ." the man who had posed as Grant Whitcomb found himself stammering. Now for the first time face to face with peril and without hordes of two-gun killers to back him up, he was panic stricken.

"Where is the girl?"

"I—I told yuh."

"You lied!" The words leaped from the Lone Ranger's lips with a crackle like that of a whip. "Now tell the truth, where is she?"

"I . . . I told yuh—the—the truth. I—I left her—"

"I'll get the truth!" The masked man quickly jammed his other gun in leather, then unhooked the heavy belts of cartridges. "Hold these," he said, passing them to Tex Wilson. Dumbly, not knowing what was to come, the Texan grasped the belt.

Then the slender figure of the Lone Ranger leaped into dazzling action. He launched himself toward the heavy man and drove a hard first with stunning force, into the small round nose. He brought his other fist around to meet the Boss's head, high on the cheek-bone. He punished the big man with a hard jab in the bulky stomach and as he bent over with a grunt and a gasp for breath, the Lone Ranger brought a fist up to meet him on the point of the chin. The fraudu-lent Grant Whitcomb would have slumped to the floor, but the masked man gripped him, holding him on his feet. "Talk," he barked, "where is Marge Whitcomb!"

"D—d—don't h—hit m—me again," begged the Boss.

"Where is she?" The Lone Ranger was spurred to a fury such as he had never known before. Here be-fore him was the leader of the fiendish killers he had trailed so long. Here, in this huge bulk of a man, was the ferocious outlaw whose followers had wiped out all the masked man's friends in ruthless and wholly uncalled for cruelty.

Now the much-feared Boss had become a sniveling coward, begging and pleading for mercy. But the Lone Ranger had no place in his heart for mercy or sympathy. Hanging would follow in due course, but first, there was an unholy satisfaction in feeling his fists punish the hateful creature whose sadistic nature brought torture and death to so many fine men of the West.

"Tell me where that girl is, or I'll beat you to within an inch of your worthless life!"

The Boss shook his head dumbly! "All right then!" he muttered. The Lone Ranger let go his hold on the big man and his knees buckled slightly. He staggered to keep his footing when again a hard driven fist caught his badly battered nose, and a crossed over hook followed at the point of his jaw. A sharp crack of bone on bone and the Boss slumped to the floor unconscious.

Breathing hard from his exertions, the Lone Ranger stepped back a pace and looked at the bulk of battered flesh in disgust. Walrus, anxious to contribute to the affair, emptied the pitcher of water over the Boss's face and head. "Fetch him around," he muttered, "so's yuh can start in where yuh left off."

But now the fury of the Lone Ranger had died down. He couldn't strike the big man again. The burning rage that had driven him before was gone.

The battered lips of the Boss were moving when the Lone Ranger buckled his six-guns in place once more. Sheriff Cook kneeled beside the Boss and heard him muttering. "D-d-don't l-let him . . . h-hit me again. D-don't let him!"

"Then talk," ordered the grim lawman. "Talk or you'll get worse than you got before."

"It-it's . . . Flynn's Cave."

"Flynn's cave! Is that where the girl is?"

The Boss nodded, then said, "Don't . . . don't let that masked man at me!"

"Flynn's Cave!" shouted the sheriff. "That's where the girl is an' if she's there she's bein' held a prisoner! That means there'll be more of the Night Legion there."

"Then," howled Walrus, "let's up an' at 'em! They's

five of us an' if we can't wipe out any fifty of them polecats—" he paused to look at the masked man who nodded his head, "then I don't know the Lone Ranger!"

The Lone Ranger was already on his way. The door ahead of him flew open and he raced for Silver. He vaulted into the saddle, while the others fumbled with the tethers of their own horses. "COME ON!" cried Sheriff Cook! He yelled to Walrus, "You stay back long enough to hog-tie that killer, then come after us." Already the masked man on the white horse was streaking in the distance. His voice trailed behind him.

"Heigh-Yo Silver, away-y-y-y."

———————

The battle at Flynn's cave was shorter than the lawmen thought it would be. They arrived in the vicinity, just in time to see the Lone Ranger charge directly into the cave despite the gunfire that came from within. The very speed and fury of the charging white stallion, carried the masked man inside the cavern before a bullet could bring him down. Once there, the rearing horse, the pounding hoofs, the slugged gun-butts and the stark surprise of the attack, kept the outlaws busy, while the lawmen closed in. The fight was over in a moment, and Marge Whitcomb was found badly frightened but quite unharmed.

Instead of heading straight back to the ranch, the girl was taken to Showdown, which was considerably nearer. She spent the night there with Sally, who was finally released from the jail, while Tonto grinned at all the things the blonde girl said to him.

The Lone Ranger and Old Walrus returned to the ranch, where with the aid of Natacha, they gave the real Grant Whitcomb every possible attention.

The next day, lawmen came to take the Boss to join his comrades at a trial preliminary to their hanging. Then it was a full week before the owner of the ranch, the real uncle of Marge and Sally, was able to sit up and realize that he was actually alive. He explained how he'd heard all that went on above the trap door. How the impostor threatened old Natacha with horrible things if she so much as breathed a word to either of the girls. He explained how he'd been kept alive so the imposter could ask questions of him, if necessary, and how Natacha had purposely put the girls in this room first and then done other small things, trying to point out that all was not just as it should be on the ranch.

The Boss had sworn to her that all her tribe would be wiped out, if she dared double cross him.

There was a great reunion in the big house when the sisters finally arrived in response to the Lone Ranger's message to them. They found their real uncle all that they'd hoped he might be. Tex Wilson's eyes were for no one but Marge, so he came with her, while Dave Sands accompanied Sally. In the week the girls had been in town, the four had become close friends, and Sheriff Cook confided to old Walrus that he'd soon have to hunt up a couple more deputies to replace the ones who seemed on the verge of marrying as soon as a couple of charming girls would consent.

There were two unoccupied chairs at the huge table that fairly groaned under its burden of food prepared by old Natacha.

The Lone Ranger and Tonto had been invited to the celebration feast, and they were there, but unseen by the others. They stood beside their horses looking in the window at the happy faces.

"We have the Night Legion," the masked man told his Indian companion, "but there are countless other outlaws to be run down and there are so many people who need Justice, that . . . well, good friend, I think as long as we've made the name Lone Ranger mean something, we can continue to help people!"

Tonto nodded, agreeable to anything his tall white friend suggested.

"I'll not unmask just yet! I want to carry on, just as the Texas Rangers would, if the Night Legion hadn't wiped them out." He mounted Silver, the mighty stallion.

At the table, Sheriff Cook lifted a wine glass and rose from his chair. "I want to give a toast tuh the man that smashed the Night Legion all tuh smithereens," he said.

The others rose to their feet. Marge gripping the hand of Tex, while Dave Sands fumbled for that of Sally. Walrus, with his mouth crammed full, was the last to get to his feet.

"To the man," said the sheriff, "who found Joe

Frisby, the man who stopped the Night Legion from getting these two girls, the man who found the glass button and the man who from the start, led us in the hunt for the Night Legion!"

"One minute!" It was the real Grant Whitcomb who spoke. "To the man," he added, "that found the way tuh put both parts of the map together! The man that showed where these girls can go to claim the birthright of their father. The Lone Ranger!"

They all drank, including old Natacha who stood just beyond the door to the kitchen. As if in response to the gesture, a call rang out on the plains and fell upon the ears of those assembled. It sounded so faintly that they were not certain whether it was real or imaginary. "Heigh-Yo Silver, away-y-y-y."

The Lone Ranger was riding with Tonto toward new adventure.

THE END

Be sure to read the next Lone Ranger Story:
"The Lone Ranger and the Gold Robbery."